His Eyes Are Blue.
Blue As The Heart Of A Flame,

Maggie thought, as the man's hand closed around hers.

Without moving, she gazed up into the stranger's eyes. They were crystal clear. They could have been cold, but they were very warm.

He was tall and trim, with the look of a man who worked outdoors. And handsome, with his longer-than-stylish dark hair and shaggy mustache. The only thing that seemed out of place was his dark blue suit.

He should be wearing jeans, she thought. Jeans, a T-shirt and a leather jacket...

Before that fantasy could take hold, she recovered her poise. "We've met before, haven't we?" she lied. "That's why I keep staring."

"No." His voice was deep, with a ragged, husky edge that was oddly appealing.

"Really? Well, I—"

"I wouldn't have forgotten, Maggie."

Dear Reader:

Spring is in the air! Birds are singing, flowers are blooming and thoughts are turning to love. Since springtime is such a romantic time, I'm happy to say that April's Silhouette Desires are the very essence of romance.

Now we didn't exactly plan it this way, but three of our books this month are connecting stories. *The Hidden Pearl* by Celeste Hamilton is part of **Aunt Eugenia's Treasures**. *Ladies' Man* by Raye Morgan ties into *Husband for Hire* (#434). And our *Man of the Month*, Garret Cagan in Ann Major's *Scandal's Child* ties into her successful **Children of Destiny** series.

I know many of you love connecting stories, but if you haven't read the ''prequels'' and spin-offs, please remember that each and every Silhouette Desire is a wonderful love story in its own right.

And don't miss our other April books: *King of the Mountain* by Joyce Thies, *Guilty Secrets* by Laura Leone and *Sunshine* by Jo Ann Algermissen!

Before I go, I have to say that I'd love to know what you think about our new covers. Please write in and let me know. I'm always curious about what the readers think—and I also believe that your thoughts are important.

Until next month,

Lucia Macro
Senior Editor

CELESTE HAMILTON
THE HIDDEN PEARL

SILHOUETTE *Desire*

Published by Silhouette Books New York

America's Publisher of Contemporary Romance

SILHOUETTE BOOKS
300 East 42nd St., New York, N.Y. 10017

Copyright © 1990 by Jan Hamilton Powell

ISBN: 0-373-05561-7

First Silhouette Books printing April 1990

Printed in the U.S.A.

Books by Celeste Hamilton

Silhouette Special Edition

Torn Asunder #418
Silent Partner #447
A Fine Spring Rain #503
Face Value #532

Silhouette Desire

*The Diamond's Sparkle #537
*Ruby Fire #549
*The Hidden Pearl #561

*Aunt Eugenia's Treasures trilogy

CELESTE HAMILTON

has been writing since she was ten years old, with the encouragement of parents who told her she could do anything she set out to do and teachers who helped her refine her talents. The broadcast media captured her interest in high school, and she graduated from the University of Tennessee with a B.S. in Communications. From there, she began writing and producing commercials at a Chattanooga, Tennessee, radio station.

Celeste began writing romances in 1985 and now works at her craft full-time. She says she "never intends to stop." Married to a policeman, she likes nothing better than spending time at home with him and their two much loved cats, although she and her husband also enjoy traveling when their busy schedules permit. Wherever they go, however, "It's always nice to come home to East Tennessee—one of the most beautiful corners of the world."

For my aunts,
Carolyn Carden and Sue Carden Gaines,
who encouraged me to love the written word
and gave me the first romance novels I ever read.

With special thanks
for the encouragement and support of my friends
in the East Tennessee Romance Writers, Inc.

One

His eyes are blue. Blue as the heart of a flame.

The fanciful observation was uncharacteristic for Maggie O'Grady. Yet she thought it again as she stood by her brother's side, facing a man Daniel had said was an old friend. The man's hand closed around hers, and the noise from her brother's housewarming party swelled, masking the introductions. It was just as well, because the polite words that formed in her throat remained unspoken. Without moving, she gazed up into the stranger's eyes. They were crystal clear. They had the potential to be cold, but now they were very warm. Her fascination with them was broken only when her brother's voice penetrated the surrounding music and laughter.

"Maggie," Daniel said, his tone suggesting this wasn't the first time he had said her name. "Maggie, are you—"

"S-sorry," she stammered. The blue-eyed stranger grinned, underscoring her embarrassment. She pulled her fingers from his grip, noting the broad, callused strength of his hand. Good Lord, what was wrong with her? She didn't normally swoon over attractive men. She had been single too long and introduced to too many men by too many well-meaning friends and relatives to swoon over anyone. Maybe she had been brooding too much over her breakup with Don. Maybe...

Daniel gave her a puzzled look. "As I was saying, Maggie, this is Jonah Pendleton, a friend of mine from college. We ran into each other unexpectedly at a meeting yesterday."

The man extended his hand again. "A pleasure, Maggie. A real pleasure." His voice was deep, with a ragged, husky edge that was oddly appealing. The voice matched his uneven yet handsome features, his longer-than-stylish dark hair and his rather shaggy mustache. The only thing that seemed out of place was his conservative, dark blue suit. He was tall and trim, with the look of a man who worked outdoors.

He should be wearing jeans, Maggie decided, her mind once again taking off on a flight of fancy. He'd look right at home in jeans and a T-shirt, with a leather jacket slung...

Before that fantasy could take hold, she recovered her poise. Daniel was still regarding her strangely, so she shook his friend's hand and attempted to explain her behavior. "We've met before, haven't we?" she lied. "That's why I keep staring."

"No."

"Really? Well, I—"

"I wouldn't have forgotten, Maggie."

It was a moment before she recognized the compliment in his softly spoken words. In that same moment her brother steered him toward the other end of the room, where Daniel's wife was waiting. Maggie noticed that Jonah limped as he walked away. The limp only made him more attractive. And mysterious, too. Halfway across the room he glanced over his shoulder at her, his blue eyes filled with appreciation. There was nothing mysterious about that bold, male appraisal.

"Well, well, well."

Those three words snapped Maggie out of whatever spell had gripped her. The unmistakable scent of Chanel made her turn to meet another pair of blue eyes. These sparkled with enough mischief to do any eight-year-old proud. Their owner, however, was eighty-one, an age at which a mischievous nature can spell real trouble.

"Aunt Eugenia," Maggie whispered in warning. "You can just take that look off your face."

"What look?"

"That who-is-he-and-when-are-you-getting-engaged look. Stop it immediately." Eugenia had become Nashville, Tennessee's most determined matchmaker.

With a show of innocence, the older woman touched a graceful hand to the gold-and-diamond necklace at her throat. Eyes opened wide in a face that was still beautiful, despite the stories of joy and heartbreak that time had written into her features. "I'm sure I don't know what kind of look you're talking about, Maggie dear."

Maggie fought to keep from smiling. Staying upset with eccentric but lovable Eugenia Davis was impossible, even though the woman's current obsession with seeing Maggie married had caused some awkward moments with men not nearly as attractive as Jonah Pendleton. Maggie glanced in his direction and was surprised—or was she pleased?—to find him still watching her.

"Oh, my," Eugenia murmured approvingly. "My, my, my."

Maggie could see the circuits switching on in Eugenia's brain. From the top of her stylishly coiffed white hair to the tips of her expensive leather pumps, the woman was transforming herself into a matchmaking machine. The effects could be disastrous to all concerned. Maggie had to stop her.

She cast about for some topic of conversation that would deflect Eugenia's attention from the man across the room. "Daniel and Cassandra's house looks wonderful, doesn't it?" Maggie gestured to the high-ceilinged, spacious room. "And this housewarming party was a good idea, particularly since they had such a small wedding and no reception."

For a moment it looked as if Eugenia wasn't going to be diverted by Maggie's chatter. Then she smiled. A cunning smile, Maggie thought with suspicion, even though Eugenia followed her lead. "I do wish Daniel and Cassandra had taken the time to have a really big wedding."

"I suppose they thought they had wasted enough time already." Maggie glanced across the room at her brother and her good friend Cassandra, a vivacious, raven-haired bride of one month. Jonah Pendleton was gone, and Cassandra was looking at Daniel as if he were the only person in the room. It seemed to Maggie that their love was a living presence, real enough to touch.

Momentary jealousy burned in Maggie's throat like acid, and she was immediately ashamed. Envy had played a small part in her life until recently. Nowadays she sometimes had to fight to keep it under control, but control it she did. "Cassandra and Daniel deserve their happiness," she said with a fierceness, as if to make up for any unkind thoughts.

Eugenia sent her a sharp glance, but nodded in agreement. "Thank goodness your brother and Cassandra finally realized they belonged together. When I consider all the years they wasted—" she clucked in disapproval "—I shudder to think where they'd be if I hadn't given them a little push." Her eyes narrowed. "Sometimes my pushing isn't such a bad thing."

"Pushing? Is that what you call it?" Maggie laughed. "I think the more accepted term is manipulation."

"You must be talking about Aunt Eugenia's matchmaking," a voice cut in. The speaker, a slender, chestnut-haired woman with eyes as blue as Eugenia's, slipped an arm around the older woman's waist. "What has my favorite great-aunt done now?"

Eugenia sniffed. "I'm your *only* great-aunt, Liz, and I've done nothing to warrant that reproachful look."

"Yet," Maggie added and grinned at her friend, Liz, who nodded in complete understanding.

"You girls have no gratitude," Eugenia grumbled. "Liz, you're forgetting that without my help you might not be wearing that diamond-studded wedding band. I was the one who brought you and Nathan together."

"Come now," Maggie protested. "Don't you think true soul mates like Liz and Nathan would have found each other anyway?"

Eugenia rolled her eyes. "Soul mates? Horse feathers! Love can always use a helping hand."

"And I'm glad you helped Nathan and me along," Liz assured Eugenia. "But why don't you give up while your luck is still holding? You've married me off and reunited Cassandra and Daniel, all in the space of a year. Why don't you let Maggie find her own man?"

Eugenia sniffed again. "Obviously Maggie needs some help. Just a minute ago she let the most divine man walk away."

"Daniel took him away."

The older woman adopted a long-suffering expression, "Now, Maggie, you could have stopped him. You know how to flirt. I taught you myself."

"Eugenia, every man I meet is not a potential mate."

"Now, Maggie—" Eugenia repeated.

"Maggie, I'd get away while the gettin's good," Liz interrupted. "It looks to me as if Eugenia's worked herself into a matchmaking frenzy tonight."

"Too bad she can't apply some of that energy to her own love life." Maggie nodded to a distinguished, gray-haired man who was threading his way through the crowd. "Eugenia, Herbert Black is on his way over here."

"Oh, blast," Eugenia muttered. "And Herbert can so cramp my style."

Liz and Maggie laughed at the woman's distress, and Maggie took that opportunity to leave. Ignoring Eugenia's entreaties to stay and chat, she ducked through the crowd. Maybe with Liz and Herbert to occupy her, Eugenia's mind could be steered onto something other than Maggie's marital status. Even if Herbert failed, Liz might succeed. She had always been more adept than any of them at handling Eugenia.

Liz was Eugenia's real great-niece, unlike Maggie and Cassandra, who merely claimed her as an honorary relative. Of course neither of them thought of Eugenia as anything other than family. Blood ties were no stronger than the love Maggie or Cassandra had for the woman, or the affection that bound all of them together.

They had been friends since their playpen days—Maggie, Liz and Cassandra. Maggie and Daniel's grandparents had lived in the same exclusive Nashville neighborhood as Cassandra's and Liz's families, and since they were all about the same age, the girls had become close friends. They had built clubhouses together, gone to the same private schools and suffered the same growing-up pains.

Eugenia had been part of their lives since they were ten, when she had ended her globe-trotting and come home to Nashville. Over twenty years had passed since the day she clattered through Liz's front door, accompanied by her devoted French maid, trunks full of treasures and the memories of a lifetime of adventures. For twenty-one years she had been their admirer and critic, confidante and taskmaster.

Twenty-one years? Could it really have been so long ago? Maggie asked herself. It seemed like only yesterday that she and her friends had sipped tea with Eugenia, pretending to be members of some obscure royal family. Oh, the stories Eugenia had told them. The dreams she had inspired. For a time, they had all been determined to run off to Europe and live just as Eugenia had lived most of her life. Eventually, encouraged by Eugenia, each had made her own dreams.

Cassandra had been the only one who ran away, to stages and studios all over the world. Just this year she had come home again and used her talent and dreams to open a performing arts school for underprivileged youths. Needy people were also Liz's concern, in her work as an attorney in the public defender's office.

And I decorate houses, Maggie thought, wondering why that seemed so flat and unappealing tonight. Most of the time she liked what she did; liked creating beautiful, livable spaces. It wasn't what she had dreamed of doing, of course. Her dreams had been much simpler— a big, old house, a garden out back, a husband, kids...

Before she could become lost in a fruitless tangle of wishful thinking, Maggie claimed a glass of champagne from the bar. She sipped her drink and occupied herself by studying the cross section of Nashvillians drifting through Daniel and Cassandra's new home.

Businessmen, politicians and society matrons mingled with songwriters, musicians and students from Cassandra's school. Maggie didn't want to be drawn into a conversation with anyone, but as she moved through the press of people, she nodded to those she knew—the lifelong friends, casual acquaintances and clients for whom she had decorated homes and offices. She caught a brief glimpse of her brother and Cassandra. Through a break in the crowd, she again spied Eugenia and Liz and Herbert Black, who had been joined by Liz's husband, Nathan Hollister.

Nowhere did Maggie see the intriguing Jonah Pendleton.

Which is just fine, she told herself. *Especially since I wasn't looking for him.* She didn't care if he was gone. She was keeping her vow not to worry about men or romantic relationships. She obviously didn't know what she wanted in that respect. If she did, she would have married Don this past summer. Don had offered her everything she had ever said she wanted. But in the end she was the one who had pulled back. So maybe it was time to reassess her goals. Maybe, as Don had said, she was lying to herself about what she was really looking for.

Thinking about her last ugly scene with Don and about the things he had said to her, Maggie twisted her fingers through the strand of pearls at her neck. These had once been Eugenia's pearls, and that made them all the more precious. Maggie wore them often, touched them often. They made her feel as if she carried a bit of Eugenia's strength and courage with her always.

"They'll break if you keep that up."

The voice was unmistakable, although Maggie was dismayed to realize she had memorized the silk-and-gravel tones of Jonah Pendleton. She found herself caught by his disturbing gaze once more, and she wondered when he had slipped up beside her.

"The pearls," he said, not waiting for her reply. "It would be a shame to see them break and disappear under this crowd's feet."

Obediently Maggie let the necklace drop back to her chest. Through the silk of her dress, the pearls felt warm and heavy. Jonah Pendleton's gaze felt the same way. The sensation made her nervous and she began to chatter, "I'm afraid fiddling with them has become a bad habit. When I'm worried or—"

"Now what would a beautiful woman like you have to be worried about?"

The teasing, flirtatious comment calmed Maggie. Despite the aura of mystery she had ascribed to this man, he was no different than many others she had met. They all had a line and a story. And she could play their game when she had to, or when she wanted to. Flirting was a game Eugenia had taught her, but over the years Maggie had made it her own. Playing along for a few moments cost her nothing. It meant less than nothing to the man involved. So she flicked her eyelashes coyly at Jonah Pendleton. "Since you don't know me, you can't be sure what I have to worry about. Perhaps I've been standing here plotting a murder."

He laughed then, a hearty sound that drew the attention of several nearby guests. Taking a sip of the drink he held, he shook his head. "In my experience, lovely ladies don't plot murders."

Maggie arched an eyebrow at him. "In your experience? Are you a cop?"

"I'm a lot closer to being a cop than you are to being a murderer."

"You're taking a lot for granted."

"Not really. You're Daniel O'Grady's sister, and unless he's changed completely since college he's just about the straightest arrow around."

"Well, you're right about that," Maggie agreed. "But brothers and sisters aren't always alike."

"Okay." The man brushed a finger across his mustache as he studied her. "Let's just say that I don't believe a woman with brown eyes like yours—an angel's eyes—could ever do anything to hurt anyone."

To her chagrin, Maggie felt a flush crawl up her neck. This conversation was nonsensical, but there was something a bit too intense about Jonah Pendleton. She glanced down at her champagne flute and sent the effervescent liquid swirling around. The bubbles rose to the surface and popped, reminding her of how fleeting encounters with men like this were, how little substance they actually had. That made her smile, and she glanced at him again. "I thought angels had blue eyes," she drawled, "like yours."

"No, no." He shook his head and grinned. "And I'm the proof. Every Sunday-school teacher I ever had referred to me as a blue-eyed imp."

"Now that I can see," Maggie retorted, laughing.

Genuine laughter transformed her, Jonah decided. Without it she was a pretty picture. But just a picture—with soft, chin-length blond hair, big, brown eyes and a generous, kissable mouth. When she laughed, though, she looked more like a woman with red blood pumping through her veins and less like a properly reared, coquettish Southern girl. She acted that part well. He had nothing against role-playing, or even propriety, as long as it didn't interfere with what he wanted. It was Jonah's opinion, however, that women in his hometown remained flirtatious girls far too long. He thought they were much more interesting when they dropped their affectations and became something more, something real. He wondered if Miss Silk-and-Pearls O'Grady might be interested in some reality. When Daniel had introduced her, there had been something in her expression—a hint of frustration?—that told Jonah she might.

An inappropriate thought about an old friend's sister, he chastised himself. There were unwritten rules about such things. One didn't play fast and loose with certain women and, unfortunately, fast and loose was the only game he had bothered to learn. With regret, he allowed his gaze to slip over the full, womanly curves Maggie's blue, silky dress displayed so well. *Maybe I'll say to hell with the rules this time,* he thought.

He was turning that possibility around in his head when their conversation was interrupted.

"Aunt Eugenia," Maggie breathed, and Jonah saw her stiffen, even though she hid her discomfiture immediately. He wondered why. Aunt Eugenia looked to him to be a harmless sort. A tiny woman, elegantly dressed, obviously wealthy. Old money, he decided as Maggie performed the introductions with just the right panache.

There was no mistaking Eugenia's intent as she gazed from Jonah to Maggie. She was pairing them off in her mind. Her bright blue eyes studied him with lively interest. "I thought I knew every attractive man in this town. You must be a newcomer."

He wasn't sure if it was the woman's unexpected bluntness or Maggie's hastily concealed impatience that made him smile. He already knew he liked Maggie best when she wasn't putting on a cool, flirtatious act. Watching her deal with Eugenia might be amusing. "I'm practically a newcomer," he said in answer to Eugenia's implied question. "I've only been home for a couple of visits since I left twelve years ago, and Nashville's changed a lot since I lived here."

"You're home to stay, I hope." Again Eugenia darted a sly glance from Jonah to Maggie and back again. Jonah caught the way Maggie's soft mouth tightened.

"I'm here for a bit to help my brother with the family construction firm," he explained.

Recognition dawned in Eugenia's face. "Your father was Roger Pendleton, wasn't he?"

"You knew him?"

"Not well. But I knew his reputation." Eugenia's gaze softened, and she placed a comforting hand on Jonah's arm. "He was a good man, my boy. A generous one, too. I head up a charity committee to benefit a summer camp for children. His company always contributed. He will be missed by many people."

The muscles worked in Jonah's jaw as he sought to make some appropriate reply to Eugenia's gracious remarks. It was still so hard to talk about his father in the past tense, even now, almost a year after his death. Maybe it would be different if Jonah had made it home for the funeral. Maybe seeing that coffin being lowered into the ground would have made his father's death a reality. But Jonah had been in another country when the news had reached him, and he had been in no shape to travel. So they had buried his father without him. And that was just one more thing he had to regret.

Eugenia patted his arm now, as if she understood why he said nothing. Jonah glanced at Maggie and found sympathy in her eyes, too. For some irrational reason, that bothered him. He didn't need pity.

He drank the last of the tequila in his glass. It burned its way down his throat, but he knew from experience it wouldn't blunt any of his pain. He muttered a gruff "Thank you" to Eugenia before starting to move away. "Now, if you'll ex—"

"You really should get reacquainted with your hometown," the older woman interjected before he could leave. "You might find you want to stay on."

"I'll just be here for a few months, probably."

She chuckled. "That's what I said when I came home from Paris two decades ago."

"Paris's loss, I believe," Jonah responded with automatic gallantry.

"How kind you are." Again, Eugenia cut her eyes toward Maggie. "A man who is handsome as well as charming. That combination is rare these days, isn't it, Maggie dear?"

"Yes, *genuine* charm is rare," Maggie retorted sharply, but immediately looked guilty when Eugenia frowned at her.

Jonah liked the flash of temper better than the guilt, and he began formulating a suitably stinging reply. Sparring with an angry Maggie O'Grady could be fun.

Eugenia, however, forestalled him. "Where are you staying while you're in town, Jonah?"

"Actually I've been at my parents' house, but I'm not really..." He paused, not knowing exactly how to explain the way his well-intentioned mother smothered him after all the years he had been on his own. "I'm looking for a place to rent for a while."

"How marvelous!" Eugenia exclaimed. "Maggie is an interior designer. I'm sure she knows something suitable that's available. Don't you, Maggie?"

Obviously holding her irritation at bay, Maggie said, "He would probably do just as well with the for-rent ads or with a real-estate agent."

Eugenia dismissed that notion with a toss of her head. "What nonsense. It's always better to have the help of someone you know." She turned to Jonah. "You do want Maggie to give you a hand, don't you?"

He grinned, noting the annoyed flush that spread across Maggie's peaches-and-cream complexion. Helping him find an apartment was the last thing she wanted to do. So perversely he agreed with Eugenia. "Who wouldn't want her help?"

"Then it's settled," Eugenia said in triumph. "You're free tomorrow, aren't you, Maggie?"

Now thoroughly amused by Eugenia's overt manipulation, Jonah watched the emotions that warred in Maggie's expression. It was clear she didn't like bucking Eugenia. It was also clear that she would love to tell the woman to go to hell. Perversely, he hoped she would. It would prove she had spirit, and he liked women with fire and flash.

But Maggie disappointed him. She schooled her expression into a polite mask and told him to call her. Then she excused herself as coolly as possible and left him standing with Eugenia. He got the feeling this was a routine she had been through before.

At his side, Eugenia heaved a sigh.

"What's wrong?" he asked her sharply. "Not pleased at the turn of events?"

If he had hoped to anger, he was disappointed. Eugenia merely chuckled. "You should be the one who is disappointed, my boy. You just struck out with a girl who is a treasure you're not likely to find everyday."

Struck out? He couldn't have. He'd been doing just fine until Eugenia had stuck her nose into it. Thoughtfully Jonah turned to watch Maggie slip out the French doors at one end of the room. Then he smiled at Eugenia. "Anybody ever tell you that you're an interfering, old busybody?"

Eugenia laughed even harder, obviously not in the least insulted. "If I listened to what everyone said, I'd never accomplish a thing."

"And what a pity that would be," Jonah observed with sarcasm. Instead of sticking around to hear Eugenia's reply, he headed for the same door Maggie had used. The older woman's laughter trailed after him.

Maggie stood on the terrace, letting the cool October breeze chase the angry warmth from her cheeks. Clouds had momentarily covered the harvest moon, and beyond the light streaming from the house's many windows, the lawn and gardens were dark. She took a deep breath. This was the first really cool spell of the season, an unseasonably cold night. Perhaps that was why the terrace was deserted.

The air smelled like autumn, like wood smoke and leaves. On cue, a few leaves danced across the terrace's brick floor. More rustled in the tall trees. In the coming weeks they would fall and form a winter blanket for the garden Cassandra had labored so hard to put in order during the past month.

Thinking of Cassandra's improbable and unexpected gardening skills, Maggie was able to forget Eugenia and Jonah Pendleton for a moment. But only for a moment. Remembering them again, she rubbed a neck that was suddenly stiff with tension. Then she tangled a hand through her pearls. She was tired. Tired of meeting men who seemed perfect and turned out to be all wrong. Tired of Eugenia's machinations. Tired of dating. Yet tired of being alone, too. God, she was so confused.

A door opened behind her and Maggie turned, not really surprised to see Jonah Pendleton. She said nothing as he came toward her.

He leaned against the low brick wall at the terrace's edge, grunting a little as he shifted his weight off the leg he favored. "You should have told her to mind her own business," he said after a few moments of awkward silence had passed. "I could tell you wanted to."

"Acting on one's every impulse isn't really advisable," Maggie replied, knowing she sounded as prim as an old-maid schoolteacher.

"Do you *ever* act on impulse?"

His skeptical tone rankled. "Not that it's any of your business—"

"I wish you'd drop the sweet-and-proper act."

Maggie turned to again study the darkened lawn and crossed her arms. "I don't know what you mean."

"Sure you do. Women like you hide your real self behind little games."

She glanced at him, startled by his perception.

He chuckled. "Come now, hasn't anyone ever called your bluff before?"

Don had come close, very recently, but Maggie wasn't about to let this man know it. "I think you're the one who's playing games, Mr. Pendleton."

"Now that's a laugh," he retorted. "I shoot straight from the hip, lady. I found out a long time ago that just being honest gets me further in life."

"Exactly where you are in life remains to be seen," Maggie snapped.

Her companion seemed delighted. "That's good. Get angry with me. You'd be better off if you'd get angry with that old coot inside, too. Maybe she'd leave you alone and let you make your own dates."

Temper flared inside Maggie. Just who did this man think he was, anyway? "Aunt Eugenia isn't an old coot. She's a bit eccentric, but she's been like a mother to me."

"And that means she can walk all over you?"

"She doesn't—"

"It looked that way to me."

Maggie gripped the rough edge of the wall for a moment while she calmed herself. Then she took a step backward. "Being rude and disrespectful to a wonderful woman just isn't my nature. Now, I'm going—"

"Just what is your nature?" Jonah muttered. "Your real nature?"

"Nothing about me is really any of your concern."

"I thought for a while tonight that I might make you my concern."

The sexy implication of his drawled remark momentarily astonished Maggie. Then a slow burn started in the pit of her stomach. "You really are quite despicable—"

"Despicable?" Laughter poured out of him. "My God, I never knew real people used that word."

Maggie turned away, prepared to make a dignified exit. To think she had found this man attractive. But he was really a Neanderthal. She had taken only a step when a strong hand gripped her shoulder and turned her around. "Now look—"

"Are you angry, Maggie dear?"

His mimicry of Eugenia's favorite endearment made Maggie wish for the courage to apply her knee sharply to his groin. She resisted, however, and attempted to shake off the hands he had placed on her shoulders. "Let me go."

He ignored her. "Come on, Maggie, get mad. Get really mad."

"You're absurd."

"Despicably absurd." He laughed again. "My, but I must upset your safe, little well-bred world. What's it like to live in that world, Maggie? Don't you ever get bored? Don't you ever want to come out and play in the real world?"

"I probably know more about the real world than you ever will," she hissed through lips that were white with suppressed anger.

Jonah knew a moment's regret at having upset her. He couldn't believe he was taking his frustrations out on her. The truth was, he didn't really like being back in Nashville, back in the world he considered so narrow. He had come here tonight, feeling disdainful of the life his college friend had built for himself. The big house. The foreign sedan in the drive. The adoring wife. The *settledness* of it all. Jonah had never wanted any of this. And he and Daniel had never been such close friends that there would be a reason for Jonah to be jealous of him now. So why it bothered him, he had no idea. Just as he had no idea why he was picking on Daniel's sister. She was obviously a sweet woman, and the world he had sneered at was the only one she knew or wanted.

He started to relax his grip on Maggie's shoulders. But then he looked toward the house. Standing in a brightly lit window watching them, was Eugenia. Her tiny, straight-backed figure was unmistakable. Her spying made him angry; angry enough to do something he hoped would shock the diamonds right off the old coot's neck.

So he kissed Maggie. He kissed her hard. With lips that forced hers to open. It was for Eugenia's benefit that he pressed his body intimately against Maggie's. But it was for his own benefit that he kept on kissing her, kept on pressing. Never in his wildest dreams would he have expected the sensation to be so sweet.

She never fought him. He felt her initial shock, but she allowed him to pull her deeper into the passion of the moment. She kissed him like a woman, a real woman, not someone who was hiding behind a game or a role.

They kissed until he couldn't help but thread his fingers through her soft hair. Until he wished for the privacy to put his hands on the full breasts that pushed against his chest. Until he grew hard and heavy from desire.

Then, as abruptly as he had kissed her, she jerked away. And for one startled, motionless moment, they stared at each other. The honesty he had asked of her earlier was there for him to see. She wanted him. Badly. As much as he wanted her.

He might have reached for her again, if she hadn't walked away. With heels tapping against the veranda's brick floor, she took precise, calm steps toward the house. She didn't hurry. She didn't look back, and she didn't slam any doors.

Staring after her, Jonah wiped his mouth on the back of his hand. The full moon peeked out from behind a cloud then, and he stared down at the lipstick stain on his hand.

"Damn," he whispered. "Maybe Nashville has something to commend it, after all."

Pretending to be fascinated by a painting on the wall near the French doors, Eugenia held her breath while Maggie brushed past her. The girl didn't even notice her, however. *Who would notice anything after being so thoroughly kissed?* Eugenia asked herself gleefully.

When Maggie had been absorbed into the crowded living room, Eugenia peered out the window again. But Jonah was gone. She chuckled, wondering if he was as dazed as Maggie had looked. Oh, but this was working out well, even if it had been an impromptu plan.

"You're up to something, aren't you?"

Eugenia turned to find Liz and Cassandra regarding her suspiciously. For their benefit, she sighed. "I was up to something, but I'm afraid it's failed."

"Maggie and Jonah Pendleton, right?" Cassandra said.

"How did you know?"

"He's a new man, isn't he? And it isn't like you to leave a stone unturned when seeking a mate for one of us."

Shrugging, Eugenia admitted, "I did think he was interesting, and I did try to nudge him and Maggie together."

Liz groaned. "Nudged, huh? What'd the poor man do? Run for the nearest exit?"

"Of course not. It was Maggie. She's bound and determined to reject any man I offer."

Cassandra linked her arm though Eugenia's. "You've got to leave Maggie alone, Eugenia. She's barely over Don."

Eugenia snorted. "He was so wrong for her."

"True," Liz agreed. "And Maggie eventually figured that out. Let her find her own way."

"Perhaps you're right," Eugenia said, sighing again.

"Now you're being sensible." Cassandra tugged her toward a nearby chair. "Why don't you sit here, and I'll go and get you a nice glass of champagne."

"And I'll bring you a plate from the buffet," Liz added.

So Eugenia settled into a comfortable chair and let herself be fussed over. Even Maggie eventually got over her pique and perched on the chair arm and talked. Others, including the always attentive Herbert Black, eventually surrounded Eugenia's chair like hangers-on at a French court. Eugenia noticed, however, that Jonah Pendleton—who hadn't left the party, after all—kept his distance. And Maggie gave him a distinctly cold shoulder.

And that was all very good, Eugenia decided. For she had pegged Jonah from the start as a man who chased the unattainable. Being a rebel and gypsy herself, she recognized the signs in someone else—the stubborn set of his jaw and the restless light in his eyes. She suspected the one way to get Jonah Pendleton to want something was to tell him he couldn't have it. And that was exactly what Maggie did every time she avoided his eyes.

Feeling very pleased with the turn of events, Eugenia surveyed her "girls." On Nathan's arm, Liz sparkled with happiness. With Daniel, Cassandra had found a focus for her fire and passion. As for Maggie . . . well, it was too early to predict, but Eugenia thought Jonah Pendleton was a contender for Maggie's heart. Maggie needed someone to light up her life, someone who was a bit of rake.

They need just one more little push, Eugenia decided, turning over possibilities in her head.

Herbert Black bent close to her ear. "Eugenia, dearest, I recognize that look on your face. You're up to something, and you promised the next match you made would be ours."

Silly old fool, she thought, even as she smiled at him. She really was becoming rather fond of Herbert. "Fetch Daniel over here, would you, Herbert, darling. And don't look so distressed—I'm not up to anything. Not anything, at all."

Two

___

Jonah had never regretted kissing a woman. Not even those with whom the experience had been less than expected. But he wished he hadn't kissed Maggie O'Grady. That was his first thought on the morning after the party. He had behaved terribly toward her, and for the life of him he couldn't remember why. It was far easier to remember the feel of her mouth opening beneath his.

"And that's the worst part of it," he grumbled as he headed downstairs for breakfast. He needed to forget Maggie O'Grady. Number one, because he would probably never see her again. Number two, because if he did, she'd probably give him a well-deserved punch in the nose.

Or the cold shoulder. Jonah grinned, thinking of all the times last night when their gazes had met and she had pretended to look right through him.

Forget it. Pausing in the hallway to the kitchen, Jonah again told himself to relegate Maggie O'Grady to hands-off status. He had enough to worry about without getting entangled with a woman like her.

His mother was in the kitchen, bustling about, pouring coffee and frying bacon. She did this every morning, even though he had told her he preferred just coffee and toast and could fix it himself. She ignored almost everything he told her and treated him just as she had when he was a teenager living at home. Much as he loved his mother, Jonah knew his frustration with her was going to start showing if he didn't get out of here soon.

He stood in the kitchen doorway, watching her plump but efficient figure hurry about. She wore blue jeans and a cotton shirt. Her short salt-and-pepper hair was tied back with a scarf. Jonah imagined she had a full day planned around the house. Carrie Pendleton stayed busy all the time. In addition to raising two sons and running a household, she had labored beside her husband, building the family firm. She was still in charge of the firm's office staff.

Jonah wished she could take it easy. Years of hard work had entitled her to some measure of security. Although that security was in real jeopardy. If the business didn't change soon, if he couldn't make his brother face reality, Pendleton Construction was going to go under. And all his mother would have left were memories. Jonah could take care of her financially, but that wasn't the way it should have been. It wasn't the way he knew his father would have wanted it.

Dammit, why was Michael gambling with their mother's livelihood?

A familiar knot of tension formed between Jonah's shoulder blades as he thought about his brother. He frowned, wondering how two people raised in the same house could have turned out so differently.

"You look like you got up on the wrong side of the bed," his mother said cheerily.

He grunted an acknowledgment, took a seat at the kitchen table and grimaced as he straightened his right leg. It ached this morning, a testimony to the amount of time he had spent on it last night.

His mother brought him a cup of coffee, concern evident in her blue eyes. "If that leg is hurting you, you should go see a specialist."

"It's on the mend, Mom. The doctor said it would take some time. I did fall off a bridge, you know."

She sniffed. "I'd feel better if you'd see that orthopedic man your uncle told you about. Those South American doctors—"

"Took care of me just fine," Jonah completed, reaching for the morning paper. He couldn't count the times he and his mother had had this conversation since he'd come home three weeks ago. He didn't like talking about the accident in which he had broken both legs and an arm and injured his right shoulder. Those injuries had kept him in a hospital bed while his father was being buried. Jonah had made it home for a brief visit a few months ago, just to see how his mother was. But when he had gone back to the road project he was engineering in South America, he had reinjured his right leg. It was after another hospital stay that he had decided to come back to Nashville to finish his recuperation.

Thankfully his mother didn't push the subject of his injuries this morning. Vigorously she began to scramble eggs. "You were late last night."

"Sort of, I guess." Jonah didn't elaborate. A discussion of the party would open up another subject he tried to avoid with his mother. He turned to the sports section of the paper and hoped she would take the hint.

"Michael called before you got up," she continued. "He said you shouldn't bother coming in today. Since it's Saturday, he's just going to go over some paperwork—"

"Which is why I should go in," Jonah muttered, dropping the paper.

"Michael said not to bother." His mother placed a plate full of eggs and bacon in front of Jonah. She sat down across from him with her own dry toast and coffee.

Shaking his head, he dug into his unwanted meal. "I think I'll go in anyway."

Carrie gave him a long, considering look. "Now, Jonah—"

"I want to help Michael, Mom."

"I know that, but he needs some time."

"To do what? Drive the business into the ground?"

"He won't do that."

"I wouldn't be so sure about that if I were you."

His mother shifted uncomfortably in her chair. "Michael's the one who's in charge, Jonah. That was decided a long time ago. If you're saying you want things to be different now, then we need to sit down and talk—"

"I'm not saying I want things different. The company is Michael's. All I want to do is help get things straightened out." Jonah reached across the table and gripped his mother's hand. "For your sake."

"Don't worry about me," she said firmly, although she gave his fingers a grateful squeeze. "Don't worry about Michael. Or the business. Worry about getting those bones mended so you can fly off to Egypt or New Zealand or wherever your next job is scheduled.''

"If you needed me, I could stay."

"And be perfectly miserable and of no use to anyone," she retorted in her no-nonsense way. "You couldn't settle in one place, Jonah. You were born with wanderlust in your heart. Why, at two years old, you wandered out of the house and went off to explore the neighborhood. You frightened the baby-sitter to death. Your father and I came hurrying home from work—''

"I think I remember Dad spanking me for that."

"Well, that was just the beginning. I'd sooner try and cage a moonbeam than ask you to stay." The twinkle in Carrie's eye belied the severity of her voice.

She and Jonah's father had always been this way—accepting of the choices their sons had made. Jonah knew neither of them begrudged him the freedom he had needed. He wished he could be as easy on himself. But even if they hadn't said so, he knew he should have been here all these years.

His mother darted him a tentative smile. "Someday you may settle down. Someday you might actually meet some suitable woman. Fall in love. Have a family."

Grunting again, Jonah reclaimed the paper. This was the other conversation he and his mother had nearly every day. One would think Michael's marriage and two daughters would be enough for the woman. She was almost as bad as Maggie O'Grady's Aunt Eugenia.

"Meet anyone nice at the party?" his mother pressed, trying and failing to sound casual.

Briefly Jonah wondered what his mother would think of Maggie. He scotched that thought, however, and turned to the apartments-for-rent section. He sent up a small prayer of thanks when the ringing of the phone prevented his mother from pursuing the subject of women. His faith in divine intervention was further strengthened when the caller turned out to be Daniel O'Grady, who just happened to own an apartment building with a vacancy. Jonah considered renting it sight unseen, but Daniel would hear nothing of that and agreed to meet him at the apartment later that morning.

At the appointed time, Jonah drew his car to a halt in front of an older home on a quiet residential street. The house was painted white, with bright blue shutters and wicker furniture on the broad front porch. Trees towered above the well-kept yard, and chrysanthemums bloomed next to the porch. The place had obviously once been a single-family dwelling, and that sense of homeyness remained.

While Jonah was standing on the front walk gazing about in appreciation, Daniel pulled up. "What do you think so far?" he asked, leading the way to the front door.

"It looks good on the outside."

"Eugenia thought you'd like it."

Jonah paused on the front steps. "Eugenia?"

"Sure. I thought I told you on the phone, she's the one who told me you needed a place."

"I thought I had mentioned it to you."

"No, but since Maggie—"

"Maggie?"

Daniel turned around. "There seems to be an echo here."

"What about Maggie?"

"She and I own this place." Looking unconcerned, Daniel opened the front door.

Jonah paused for a moment before following him inside. *Eugenia,* he thought. *That sly old fox.* She was orchestrating this whole thing.

Thus forewarned, Jonah wasn't surprised to see Maggie open the door to the apartment on the first floor. But he was surprised by the jolt of desire just seeing her sent through him.

That desire didn't fade, even when her stunned expression changed to one of dislike. Even when she demanded hostilely, "What are you doing here?"

Maggie pressed harder than necessary on the cover of the automatic coffee grinder until a faint electrical smell made her realize she had ground the coffee beans into a worthless powder. She muttered the most graphic curse she knew as she dumped the coffee into the trash, measured beans and started over. While the coffee brewed, she vented her frustration on the plates she unloaded from the dishwasher. The clatter of dishes reminded her of what she would love to do to Eugenia's head.

It was easy to see the older woman's fine hand in Jonah Pendleton's appearance on Maggie's doorstep. At this very moment he was looking at the small, furnished apartment on the second floor. It was the same apartment Maggie had just yesterday told Eugenia was vacant. Eugenia had been hinting about that apartment last night when she suggested Maggie help Jonah find a place to rent. Maggie was surprised Eugenia hadn't taken over and rented the apartment to him then and there. Although perhaps that would have been a trifle obvious. Even for such a shameless schemer as Eugenia. Instead she had brought Daniel in on the act.

"I'm going to tell her off, once and for all,' Maggie said, reaching for the telephone. She stopped before picking it up. For someone as nosy and interfering as Eugenia, the cruelest punishment would be to leave her in the dark about what was happening.

Maggie emptied the pot of coffee into an insulated pitcher and poured herself a cup. She stared out the window above the kitchen sink, absentmindedly noting that her favorite maple tree's leaves were changing to orange, just as they had every year of her life. The familiar sight restored Maggie's habitual calm. She had been letting things get to her too much lately, and that was unlike her. Instead of getting upset about Eugenia, it might be best to pretend unconcern. No doubt Eugenia had enjoyed stirring Maggie up. She might lose interest in her matchmaking games if Maggie acted as if she didn't care.

"I could even pretend to be friendly to Jonah Pendleton," Maggie mused. As distasteful as that notion was, she knew it would probably get Eugenia off her back. "Even putting up with that caveman will be worth a little peace." She refused to think about what had happened with that caveman last night. His kiss and the way she had responded weren't important. It had been a moment, a mere heartbeat out of their lives. It would never be repeated.

She felt a momentary flash of regret, but Maggie didn't pause to examine that emotion. Instead, she bustled around her sun-filled kitchen, putting zucchini bread and homemade jam on the round wooden table. She set out her favorite pottery coffee mugs just as Daniel called her name from the living room.

"Come on back to the kitchen," she invited cheerfully. Mentally she prepared to be polite and pleasant to Jonah Pendleton. With coffeepot in hand she turned from the counter, intending to make a breezy offer of something to eat and drink. She stopped when she looked, *really* looked, at Jonah.

Earlier in the front hall, she had been too irritated by his presence to notice the worn blue jeans or black T-shirt he wore. She noticed them now, especially the way the hand he had shoved in his jeans pocket pulled the denim tight across the distinctly male juncture of his thighs. She noticed the brown leather jacket he had thrown negligently over one shoulder. The clothes and the cocky, male pose suited him well, just as she had known they would. Just as she had *imagined* they would last night. For a woman who professed to like men in three-piece suits, she found herself approving of the way he looked. Heartily.

She's even prettier today, Jonah decided as Maggie clutched her coffeepot and stared at him. Her blue jogging suit was faded. Her hair was tousled and haloed in gold against the window. Her soft pink mouth was devoid of lipstick. But the casualness suited her, just as this cluttered, homey room suited her. Maybe she wasn't the silk-and-pearls social butterfly he had pegged her as last night.

Beside him, Daniel cleared his throat and Maggie moved forward. "Come in, come in," she said, gesturing toward the table. "I've got some coffee and bread—"

"Are you sure?" Daniel asked, frowning. "Earlier, you seemed—"

"Grouchy, I know," she completed for him. "You know how I can be in the mornings, Daniel."

Daniel looked as if he didn't know anything of the kind, but he sat down at the table anyway. Jonah followed him, favoring his stiff leg and tossing his jacket over the arm of the fourth chair at the table.

"I'm sorry if I seemed rude earlier, Jonah," Maggie continued as she poured coffee for the two men. "I just didn't expect to see you."

"No problem." He accepted a steaming mug and smiled at her. Her gaze skittered away, and her movements seemed jerky as she pulled a chair out from the table.

"I called this morning," Daniel said. "I was going to let you show Jonah the apartment."

"I was out walking over at the high-school track."

Daniel, who was busy spreading butter and jam on a piece of bread, chuckled. "I thought speed-walking was Liz's thing."

She grinned, and for the first time Jonah noticed the dimple that creased her right cheek. "I said I was walking," she said. "I didn't say anything about speed."

"Maybe it was just as well that you were out," Daniel replied, suddenly serious. "Jonah told me you and he . . . umm . . . well . . . that you had a little disagreement last night."

She finally looked Jonah square in the eye and flushed a little. "You told Daniel we . . . *disagreed*?"

Jonah sat forward, cupping his hands around his warm mug as he studied Maggie. While they had been looking at the vacant apartment, he had felt compelled to offer Daniel an explanation for the way Maggie had greeted him. He hadn't told him about the kiss. Hell, they might all be adults, but Daniel was her brother. Being attracted to a man's sister was one thing, but you didn't discuss details with him. That was an unwritten rule even Jonah wouldn't break. Especially when the details were as hot as last night's kiss.

He shifted in his chair, concentrated on a point just above Maggie's shoulder and offered an apology. "Our *disagreement* was my fault, Maggie. And I'm sorry."

She expelled a long breath. He couldn't tell what that signified, but she did say, "Apology accepted."

"So would it bother you if Jonah moved in?" Daniel asked her.

Jonah began to protest, "I don't—"

"It wouldn't bother me at all," Maggie interjected. Her brown eyes, now as cool as they'd been last night, met Jonah's again. "It'll be good to have the apartment rented without even advertising it."

He was surprised. After what had passed between them on Daniel's veranda, he had figured the lady wouldn't want him around. Hell, after what had happened last night, *he* shouldn't want to be around *her*. He had decided that this morning.

"So is it a deal?" Daniel asked him.

Jonah hesitated a second more, then nodded. "It is a nice apartment. Nicer than my usual temporary accommodations."

Maggie arched an eyebrow. "And what kind of accommodations are those?"

"Whatever my company decides to book me in." He went on to explain that he worked for an international engineering firm.

"We build roads and bridges in out-of-the-way places. One year I may be living in luxury in a pagoda of my own. The next I'm sharing a World War II Quonset hut with snakes and spiders."

"Sounds... interesting," Maggie murmured.

"Oh, it's very... interesting," he replied, amused by her description. He glanced around the room, at the ruffled curtains covering the windows, the cozy fireplace, and the framed photos that crowded the mantel. He drew in a deep breath of the spice-scented air. "You don't get to settle down in one place, though. Especially not in a house like this."

Maggie's chin lifted defensively. "Daniel and I grew up in this house."

"It's a beautiful place," Jonah assured her, hoping she believed his sincerity. He hadn't intended to sound critical of the place she lived or the way she lived. He wasn't looking for a repeat of last night's confrontation.

Daniel had edged back in his chair. His gaze was brooding as it traveled around the room. Rather than the happy, successful man he had become, for a moment Daniel looked more like the silent, pensive guy Jonah remembered from college. "Maggie's the one who gets the credit for making this place shine," he said. "It wasn't beautiful when we were kids."

He looked at Maggie, and it seemed to Jonah that a special communication passed between brother and sister. They smiled at each other as Daniel continued, "We cut the place up into apartments about—" he looked at Maggie for confirmation "—ten years ago, wasn't it? Just after—" He broke off, with an uncertain glance in her direction.

"Yes, ten years ago," she murmured and looked down at her coffee.

After what? Jonah wanted to ask. Whatever it was put shadows in Maggie's eyes and turned down the corners of her pretty mouth. He didn't push the issue. Instead, he helped himself to a slice of her bread and talked about inane subjects such as when he was moving in and the weather. But all the while he found himself wondering what had happened ten years ago that could still make Maggie look as if the world had cracked open.

He and Daniel were standing at the back door, saying their goodbyes when Daniel's wife came in through the living room. Cassandra was talking nonstop to a woman Jonah remembered from last night's party. They looked at him and exchanged a conspiratorial smile he didn't quite understand.

They've been talking to Eugenia, Maggie fumed to herself as Liz and Cassandra said hello to Jonah. Why else would they be grinning at him like a pair of fools? She told herself to remain unconcerned, to play it cool. What she really wanted to do was scream. With Liz and Cassandra now in on the act, this matchmaking campaign was officially out of control.

"We came to get Daniel," Cassandra said, taking her husband's arm.

Daniel looked confused. "But I—"

"We're going to that auction, remember?" Liz cut in.

"To look for furniture for the condominium Liz and her husband are buying," Cassandra explained, looking at Maggie as if she dared her to protest. "And we've got to go." When Daniel started to protest she tugged him toward the door. "We're late right now, darling."

"And I can't miss it," Liz added when Daniel attempted another feeble protest.

If Maggie hadn't been so irritated, she might have felt sorry for her poor, double-teamed brother. Liz herded him through the doorway while Cassandra paused to call out a saucy, "See you two."

And then they were gone. Leaving Maggie and Jonah alone.

They stood where they had remained during the entire disruption, on either side of the back door. In the sudden silence they stared at each other. The clock ticked. The refrigerator made ice. And Maggie's blood boiled.

"I'm sorry," she began.

Jonah silenced her with a dismissing gesture. "It's not your fault."

"But they're acting crazy," she protested. "All of them—Eugenia, Liz and Cassandra. It's as if we're all caught in this vaudevillian comedy. They're all running around trying to make me into a couple, as if I'm going to lose the family fortune or something if I don't settle down with someone."

"Just someone?" Jonah asked, pretending to be insulted. "You mean there's nothing special about me in particular."

Maggie chuckled, pleased to see he was taking this all in stride. "No offense, but at this point, I do believe they think any man will do."

"And what do you think?"

She rubbed the toe of her sneaker across the welcome mat, pondering the question. Then she smiled up into those startling blue eyes of his. "I think they all should just get off my case. Because I'll know the right guy when he comes along."

Jonah smiled, too, and caught her hands in his own. "You know something, Maggie dear," he drawled. "It might just be to our advantage to give everybody what they want."

"What do you mean?"

He brought one of her hands to his mouth, and his mustache tickled her skin as he pressed a kiss in her palm. "Maybe," he whispered, "just maybe you're looking at the right guy."

Three

Huh?'' It probably wasn't the most original comeback of her life, but Maggie wasn't sure she had heard Jonah correctly. The only thing that seemed real was the touch of his mouth against her palm. So she snatched her hand away and tried to clear her brain. "What did you say?"

Jonah's grin was teasing. "Let's give 'em what they want. Let's be a couple."

"You can't be serious."

"Sure I am." He shifted from foot to foot and grimaced slightly. "Could we talk about this sitting down? My bum leg's giving me a fit today."

"Oh." Maggie's gaze slid down the length of his right leg, wondering what the problem was. The leg looked okay. No, better than okay, with firm, strong-looking thighs—

"Maggie?"

Her attention snapped back to his face. He grinned, as if he knew exactly what she had been thinking. She struggled for a nonchalant reply. None came.

"Can we sit down?"

"Of course, I'm sorry. I'm just...just not thinking." *Which is the way I always end up around you,* Maggie added silently. She led the way back to the table, pulled out his chair, offered him more coffee and generally fussed over him until he once again caught her hand in his.

"Maggie, sit down."

She obeyed, choosing the chair farthest from his.

His smile was a flash of white beneath his mustache. "You look about as thrilled as Little Red Riding Hood facing the Big Bad Wolf."

Maggie forced herself to relax. "You keep catching me by surprise."

His brows drew together in a sudden frown. "I am sorry about last night's...uh...umm..." As he struggled for the right word, two spots of color appeared in his cheeks.

The flush amazed Maggie. It didn't fit her caveman image of him at all. She decided to help him out of his descriptive dilemma. "How about if we call it an encounter?"

"Right." He grinned again. "I'm sorry it happened. I behaved badly, but that aunt of yours was peeking out a window, watching us—"

"Eugenia? You're kidding?" Maggie struck the tabletop with her fist. "God, that makes me angry."

"Me, too. That's why I—" he paused, looking sheepish "—that's why I did what I did. I wanted to set her back on her heels."

"But you don't know Eugenia. She wasn't shocked. Instead, you played right into her hands."

"So maybe we should keep on playing."

She was momentarily startled. Did he mean— "Not that we should repeat last night," he said hurriedly. "I meant what I said earlier about it not happening again."

It. What a nondescript word for that kiss we shared, Maggie thought. Nevertheless, she nodded.

"But I also meant what I said about becoming a couple."

"A couple with no...uh...encounters."

"Exactly. We *pretend* to be a couple. All your friends are happy. They leave you alone. You're happy."

Maggie slid her hands along the smooth surface of her table and regarded the man across from her with suspicion. "Exactly what do you get out of this pretense?" Several strange and unsavory possibilities were presenting themselves in her mind. "Don't tell me you'd do this for nothing."

"Hey, I have people on my back, too, you know." He counted them off on his fingers. "My mother, my aunts, my grandmother, a whole passel of cousins. None of them can understand why a thirty-three-year-old man hasn't settled down. They can't accept that I'm just not the settling kind."

"Haven't you told them that?"

He chuckled. "In my family, words are sometimes ignored. They always require proof."

"And I could prove something to them?"

"Sure. If we spend time together while I'm here in Nashville, they'll leave me alone. They'll stop fixing me up with everybody's best friend's sister's cousin."

Maggie had to giggle. "With me it's always so-and-so's brother's accountant's nephew."

"They act as if we're desperate or something, don't they?"

"We're supposed to be desperate."

"So why aren't you?"

His blunt question caught her off guard. "I beg your pardon?"

He held up a calming hand. "Now don't go getting all riled up at me again. It's just that you seem like the settling kind. Women like you are usually married or looking pretty hard."

Maggie was a person who didn't get angry in a hurry. Cassandra liked to say she had the patience of a priest hearing confessions. She was slow to be startled. She could always be counted on for a reasonable response. Yet this man had proven he could touch off her anger faster than fire licking through dry weeds. "Women like me?" she repeated in a tight voice. "You're into generalizations, aren't you?"

Jonah realized his mistake immediately. "I'm sorry," he said, then laughed. "I seem to be apologizing to you all the time."

Her brown eyes were chilly. "Doesn't bode well for a pretend couple, does it?"

"I'll do better," he assured her. "We just don't know each other very well. That's why I was asking—rather badly, I admit—why you aren't interested in...uh...well, in a relationship."

"I never said that."

"But, I got the impression last night that..." Jonah paused as the telltale flush of anger bloomed in her cheeks. Leaning back in his chair, he ruffled a hand through his hair. "I'm not doing very well, am I?"

"That depends what you're trying to do. Now, if you're trying, as you did last night, to get me really, really mad—"

"I'm not. Truly I'm not, but Maggie..." He leaned forward. "I mean, I'm not a conceited fellow, but I'm not chopped liver, either. Yet you're not interested. There must be a reason why."

The corners of her mouth twitched. "Maybe I just don't like you. Ever think of that?"

Unconvinced, he grinned back at her. "Maggie. Now come on. You like me a little. I know that for a fact." His gaze dropped to the soft, pink lips he could so clearly remember kissing last night. Whether she liked him or not, she had liked that kiss. Liked it a great deal. He wished he had liked it a little less. Just the memory made him want to kiss her again.

His gaze lifted, and she colored under his regard. She was remembering kissing him, too. It showed in the velvety brown depths of her eyes, in the way she tried and failed to look away. No, she might not like him, but she certainly wasn't indifferent to him, either. That pleased some masculine need deep inside him, and he smiled.

Maggie frowned in response. "No, Jonah Pendleton, I really can't say that I like you."

"I thought we were getting along rather well last night before Eugenia got in on the act."

"In your opinion maybe. I didn't—"

"Okay, okay." He threw his hands up in defeat. "I stand corrected. When we met there was no chemistry between us at all. At least not on your part. I, on the other hand, always react to a beautiful woman."

The dimple which had begun to appear in her right cheek disappeared. "This is probably part of the reason I don't like you."

Muttering in disgust, he rested his elbows on the table and propped his head in his hands. "You're cruel, Maggie, really hard. Here I am with this busted leg, and you further damage my fragile male ego."

She burst out laughing. "Your ego is in fine shape."

Her laughter was a good sign, but Jonah didn't raise his head to look at her. Morosely he muttered, "You can't know that."

"Yes I can," she returned, still chuckling. "And your limp is actually very attractive."

He looked up then. "You think so? You actually find something about me attractive? Then you can't really hate me, can you?"

"No, I don't hate you." Maggie decided it was impossible to truly dislike someone who could laugh at himself.

"Well, if you don't hate me, then there's no reason why we can't go forward with my plan."

"I wouldn't say that."

He sat back. "Why?"

She shrugged. "Because it's silly, and it probably won't work."

"Of course it will work. I know how to pretend to have a relationship. I've done it before." Again, his smile flashed. "Unintentionally, of course."

He made her laugh, and she believed him. Jonah Pendleton certainly didn't seem like the kind of man who made serious commitments. How could he when he was always on the move? Thoughtfully, Maggie reached for one of the coffee mugs and contemplated the smooth, blue-glazed pottery. The color reminded her of Jonah's eyes. She glanced up to find him watching her with a bemused expression. "What is it?"

"You are beautiful, you know. I thought so from the first time I saw you last night."

"Compliments aren't necessary." Avoiding his gaze, Maggie stood and carried the mugs to the sink.

His voice dropped lower and took on the gravelly edge that set off a chain reaction in the pit of her stomach. "It wasn't a *necessary* compliment. I meant it. You're a lovely woman. Intelligent, too, from what I've seen. In fact, I can't imagine why your friends are having to play matchmaker."

She couldn't dispute the sincerity in his voice, so she turned from the sink, feeling rather ashamed of her ungracious treatment of him. "Thank you," she said simply.

Once again Jonah looked around the room where they sat. It was a place that said "home, sweet home" better than any needlepoint sampler she might have placed on the wall. And there were several of those. Just as there were comfortable chairs in front of the fireplace and an ottoman on which to put up one's feet at the end of a long day. It was the kind of room a person might get used to coming home to. Maggie was the same kind of woman. If, of course, one wanted to come home to someone. He didn't, but there were many who did. He couldn't imagine she was unattached for any reason other than choice.

"Tell me," he asked, selecting his words carefully. "Why is it you've chosen not to be involved with someone?"

She didn't take affront, but she, too, seemed to deliberate over her words. "When you've made a mistake, you're pickier the second time around."

"We all make mistakes."

She paused, took a deep breath and met his eyes. "But mistakes that end in divorce are different."

"You're divorced?"

"For almost ten years."

Ah, Jonah thought, *the ten-year-old cataclysm that had upset her earlier.* His brows drew together in a frown. Ten years ago she had been so young. Too young. Her husband had probably been her first love. Maybe that was why the divorce still seemed like a tragedy to her.

"Don't look so surprised," she admonished him with a gentle smile. "Death, divorce, disappointment—all part of the real world, Jonah. I told you last night I knew something about it."

He was embarrassed, remembering the taunting remark he had thrown at her. She was really very different than he had imagined. "Last night I was a horse's ass, Maggie."

"That's a little strong, but you're close."

"You know, I'm more convinced than ever that we should enter into a partnership. I like the real Maggie."

"Real?"

"The woman who flirted with me last night wasn't real."

Maggie crossed her arms and settled back against the counter. "Oh, she's a part of me."

"I'll take your word for it, but I like this Maggie the best." He got to his feet and crossed the room to lean against the counter beside her. "So come on, have we got a deal? We could even have some fun, watching everyone watching us."

"That is tempting."

"Let's do it—as friends."

Maggie was certain she shouldn't agree. It would be nice to put one over on Eugenia and her friends, but there was something about Jonah Pendleton. Something that told her she might be tempted to forget the pretense if they spent too much time together. And that would be terrible. He was a temporary sort of man. She was a permanent sort of woman. If she became too intrigued with him, she would give him the weapons necessary to hurt her. Yet— "Just think," he murmured. "You could have several months free of Eugenia's annoying little tricks."

That knowledge and Jonah's teasing smile were too enticing for Maggie to resist. The danger of falling for him was minimal, anyway, she decided. Nothing could happen. He wasn't really interested in her, nor she in him. Her fears were groundless. She put out her hand. "It's a deal."

"Fantastic." His hand closed around hers.

His grip was strong. His hand, as she remembered, was hard and somewhat callused. Touching him, even casually, was pleasant.

She thought she saw a spark of the same interest in his eyes. But she couldn't be sure. For in the next instant he dropped her hand and moved toward the door.

"We'll start this thing tomorrow," he said. "I'll move in tomorrow morning, and we'll go have Sunday dinner at my grandmother's at . . ." He faltered, as if he realized he was giving orders. "What I meant to say was, if you're not busy tomorrow—"

"I'm not," she replied, grinning.

"Then will you please have dinner with me at my grandmother's?"

"A family dinner?"

"Of course."

"With your mom and your aunts in attendance?"

"They make their favorite recipes and gather there at least once a month."

"Gonna prove something to them, huh?"

His smile was brilliant. "Sunday dinner's always at one. We'll need to leave about twelve-thirty. Grandmother lives out from the city, toward Murfreesboro."

She nodded, and he went out the back door. Maggie watched him pass the side windows as he walked down the driveway to the front of the house. He disappeared from her view, and she turned with a sigh, her gaze falling on the jacket he had left on one of her kitchen chairs. She picked it up, intending to go after him. Instead, following some impulse, she lifted the jacket to her face.

The brown leather was worn, soft against her skin. It smelled of Jonah. A trace of tobacco. A hint of aftershave. The scents were subtle, yet masculine. They reminded her of last night's kiss, the coaxing pressure of his lips, the lingering taste of liquor in his mouth. Funny, but she had never found that taste to be pleasant before.

The phone rang and Maggie jumped, dropping the jacket almost guiltily. "You idiot," she admonished herself as she snatched it off the floor. But she was breathless when she answered the phone.

"Maggie dear, did I catch you at a bad time?"

It was Eugenia, and her too-innocent tone made Maggie grin. "Actually, Eugenia, I just said goodbye to Jonah."

"Jonah?" Eugenia's voice held gentle inquiry, as if she were trying to place the name.

Maggie resisted the urge to hang up the receiver. "You know—Jonah Pendleton—you met him last night and sent him over here with Daniel to rent the apartment."

"Oh yes, Roger Pendleton's boy."

"Yes, that boy," Maggie replied dryly, thinking the title was the last one she would give to Jonah. Then she grinned. "You know, Eugenia, I have to thank you for that."

Her hesitation was slight but detectable. "You do?"

"He's very interesting. I'm having dinner with him tomorrow."

There was a moment of silence. Then Eugenia cleared her throat. "That's nice—"

"Yes, well, gotta run now. Lots of things to do, you know." Maggie barely replaced the receiver before her laughter bubbled over. Jonah was right. This could be fun.

The Sunday afternoon scene was cut from Jonah's childhood memory book. There was the big brick house set back from the road, the cars lining the driveway, and the youngsters spreading out over the broad front lawn. Twenty-some years before, he had been with them—he and his brother and his cousins. Now, it was his brother and his cousin's children who ran and laughed and tussled in the warm autumn sunshine.

Guiding his rental car up the drive, he sensed rather than saw Maggie lean forward in the seat beside him. "What a wonderful place to live."

Jonah glanced from the house to her appreciative face. "I guess." He had never really considered the merits of living here. This was simply his grandparents' house.

"It's like living in the country."

"Not quite." He pointed to the new houses under construction across the road. "Nashville's progress marches on. I remember when that was an empty field. We waged some magnificent softball games there."

"Look at it this way, progress must be good for the family construction business."

But not good enough, he added silently. Rather than dwell on that depressing thought, he pointed to the creek that edged the sloping backyard. A small wooden bridge crossed to the woods beyond. "Speaking of construction. There's my first bridge, still standing after twenty years."

"Your first?"

"There are four others on two continents."

"I'm impressed."

He pretended shock. "You can't mean it. Maggie O'Grady, impressed with me?"

"Don't get cocky. It won't last."

They were laughing as they got out of the car, but Jonah saw Maggie hesitate when he reached in the back seat for the cake she had baked and insisted on bringing. She smoothed a hand over the waistband of her full blue cotton skirt. Then she tugged at the lacy collar of the matching blouse. "Jonah, are you sure this is a good idea?"

He smiled his encouragement. "It'll be okay. All you have to do is pretend to like me a little. That'll keep them happy, and they'll do most of the talking."

Before Maggie could reply, they were surrounded by children. At least ten of them. All looking to be under nine years old. They were all talking, but the smallest, a little girl, was the only one who made herself heard. "Unca Jonah," she screamed and proceeded to wrap her arms around his good leg.

The cake container tilted in his hands and would have fallen if Maggie hadn't grabbed for it.

"Watch out, small fry." He caught another little girl before she could glue herself to his bad leg.

The back door banged open then, and they were soon enveloped by more children and grown-ups. It was a little like going into a swarm of bees, Maggie decided, as she was relieved of her cake and propelled inside the house. And Jonah had been right. There was no need to be nervous. The fact that she had arrived with him seemed to ensure her automatic acceptance. She had been worried about what would be required of her as his pretend girlfriend, but she needn't have bothered. Jonah stuck close to her side and introduced her to everyone. Still, it was impossible for Maggie to remember the names that went with all the faces.

His paternal grandmother was one of the few it was easy to single out. Like her grandson, she was tall and lean, and she seemed quite undisturbed by the crowd that had taken over her house. She was used to crowds, she told Maggie. Jonah's father had been the only son of a family of six children. Now even her grandchildren had offspring, and almost everyone was in attendance to welcome Jonah home today.

With all these people, this family to love him, Maggie found herself wondering why Jonah had ever wanted to leave. To her, it seemed like a dream come true.

His brother, Michael, arrived late, just after the blessing had been said and everyone was moving through the buffet line that had been set up in the kitchen. Maggie decided Michael was really the more handsome of the two brothers. His features were regular where Jonah's weren't perfectly so. His hair was of a conventional length and style. He was even taller and broader of shoulder. The two little girls who had greeted Jonah earlier turned out to be Michael's daughters, and one of the many attractive women Maggie had met was his wife.

Jonah introduced Maggie to his brother, then cuffed him lightly on the arm. "It's not like you to be late for one of Grandmother P's spreads."

Michael muttered something about "business" and excused himself, leaving Jonah with a faint frown and Maggie with the feeling that all was not well between the men.

She didn't dwell on her suspicions, however. By the time she had made it through the buffet line, she was glad to sit with Jonah at a table on the screened-in porch and eat. His mother sat across from them, the blue eyes that were so like his sparkling with curiosity.

"So I understand Jonah is renting an apartment from you, Maggie?"

Before Maggie could answer, he casually draped an arm around her shoulders. "Lucky me, don't you think, Mom?"

"Well, you were welcome to stay with me, but—" her gaze slipped to Maggie again and became even warmer "—I believe I understand why you had to move, son."

Maggie felt a bit uncomfortable and busied herself by slicing into a piece of baked ham. She didn't want Jonah's mother thinking they had gotten too chummy. After all, they'd only known each other two days. "I guess Jonah told you that he knows my brother."

"My, yes. He explained everything to me last night."

There was something in the woman's broad smile that made Maggie wonder exactly what Jonah had included in his explanation. She got no answers from him. All he did was squeeze her shoulder. Then he smiled in the teasing way she was becoming accustomed to.

His mother's pleasure radiated across the table. Looking up, Maggie found herself the object of other beaming faces. For the first time she realized Jonah's problem really did compare with the one she had with Eugenia. In fact, his might even be a little worse.

Feeling sorry for him, she placed her hand on his arm as she asked him to pass her the pepper. Then she let her hand linger on the warm skin below his rolled-up shirt-sleeve, and she looked at him with what she hoped was a properly love-struck expression. He smiled in response, and she could actually feel the ripple of approval that spread around the porch.

Their approval was magnified when someone sliced into the Italian cream cake Maggie had brought. An aunt with even less tact than Eugenia stopped by Maggie's table and patted her on the shoulder while eyeing Jonah. "A beautiful girl who can also cook. You could do worse, Jonah, my boy."

The afternoon continued in much the same way. A touch-football game was organized on the front lawn. Maggie and Jonah and many others watched from the sidelines. Clearly frustrated by his inability to play, Jonah became involved in the game, yelling out pointers, alternately cheering and chastising his cousins.

He's so absolutely male, Maggie thought, watching his features come alive with excitement and pleasure. Like half his male cousins and most of his uncles, he smoked an after-lunch cigar. Smoking was near the top of her list of pet peeves, but the activity looked altogether different on Jonah. With the cigar clenched between his teeth and the breeze ruffling through his too long dark hair, he reminded her of a pirate. Or a riverboat gambler. Or maybe an outlaw. He made her think of every improbable, secret fantasy she had ever had about impossible, unsuitable men. Those thoughts sent excitement tiptoeing up her spine, and she shivered.

In response, Jonah put his arm around her shoulders and then leaned over to say something to the cousin who sat on her other side. The movement brought them close. His chest was firm against her arm as he drew her against him. His voice was a husky murmur. His scent was soap-and-water clean yet distinctly male.

She told herself those were things she might notice about any man who was seated so close. She thought her stomach would flutter if any man teased her, ruffled her hair or kissed her on the cheek as Jonah did next. Irritated by her traitorous reactions, she reminded herself he was just playing his part. And no matter how she felt about them, his actions achieved the desired results. His relatives gazed at them happily.

All but one.

Jonah's brother watched them with something less than cheer. Nearly every time Maggie looked at Jonah, she saw Michael in the background, staring at them with a frown. He sat with his wife, and when Maggie walked past them on her way to the bathroom in the house, she caught a comment she was sure she was meant to overhear.

"Looks like the prodigal son brought home a princess this time."

The bitter resentment in the man's voice brought Maggie up short, but when she looked at him, Michael was gazing in the opposite direction. His wife's attention was fixed on one of their daughters, who had run up to ask a question.

Maggie continued on her way, wondering what it was between the brothers that would cause such antipathy.

Michael's attitude was the only discordant note in a seemingly harmonious family.

Because everyone else was so very pleasant, she did her best to dismiss Michael from her mind. Maggie allowed herself to be seduced by this American-dream family. They made it easy to imagine she was a part of them. Jonah's attentiveness made it easy to forget she was putting on an act. At the end of the day she didn't want to go home. And when they got home, she didn't want Jonah to leave.

"Please come in," Maggie urged as they crossed the porch that led to her back door. "We need to have a glass of wine and drink a toast to the successful launching of our project. Now if we can just fool Eugenia." Maggie unlocked the door and turned to smile up at Jonah. "Perhaps we need to plot our strategy for that. Please stay."

Jonah knew he should go. But Maggie made an appealing picture as she posed there in her doorway. Too damn appealing. Even as he was telling himself to run, he followed her inside.

She chatted about the day while she rummaged through cabinets, getting out wineglasses, finding a corkscrew. Late afternoon shadows were filling the room, so Jonah switched on a lamp and lowered himself into one of the chairs beside her fireplace. The soft cushions were kind to his aching muscles. "Just as comfortable as I imagined," he muttered.

Maggie turned from the refrigerator. "What?"

"Nothing." Groaning, Jonah eased his leg up on the ottoman. It was comfortable, too. He closed his eyes and gave in to his aches and pains, letting Maggie's sweet voice form a pleasant background.

"You overdid it today, didn't you?"

Jonah's eyes flew open. Maggie, her face full of concern, had perched on the edge of the ottoman in front of him. Her skirt was brushing his jeans leg. Her legs were almost touching his left knee. She held two glasses and a bottle of wine. The smile on her face was tentative. "Your mother told me today how you fell off that bridge in South America. You should go easy on this leg."

He shifted the leg away from her, grimacing at the resulting pain. "It's fine, really. I'm supposed to get plenty of exercise."

Maggie looked doubtful. "Jonah, if you'd rather go home and give it a rest—"

"Nonsense. I'm resting here." He took the wine from her. Against the cold bottle their fingers met for an electrifying second, but Jonah ignored the sensation— just as he'd been ignoring similar jolts all day long. Instead he busied himself by unscrewing the cork and filling the glasses.

He set the wine bottle on the floor and took the glass Maggie offered. A toast was in order, something that would diffuse this intensity between them. "How about—to us?" he offered hastily, then wished he could recall the words, even as his glass touched Maggie's. The toast was too intimate, just as this woman with her shining brown eyes was too sweet, the wine too mellow and the tightening of his body too quick.

Thankfully Maggie moved from the ottoman to the other chair, and his head cleared and his body again relaxed. She was quiet for a moment, and he realized that was one of the qualities he liked best about her—her ability to be silent. She had been quiet many times today, sitting back, watching his family. Many women would have said too much, tried to be witty, but Maggie had been comfortably calm.

Comfortable. Damn, there was that word again. Just being with Maggie was too *comfortable*. He watched her shift sideways in her chair, drawing one leg up under the other, making herself comfortable. He smiled at his choice of words, and let his gaze follow the movement of her fingers as they threaded through her shining, blond hair. He remembered the feel of that hair against his fingers. Soft as a child's.

She smiled at him as she leaned her head against the back of the chair. "I liked your family a lot, Jonah."

"I think we're too big to be called a family. We're more like a clan."

"Clan—family—whatever. They're all nice. I wasn't sure families like that still existed."

"Don't you have a similar one? There's Aunt Eugenia."

Maggie shook her head, explaining the relationship she had with Eugenia, Liz and Cassandra. "I guess they are my family. With Daniel, of course."

"What about your parents?"

A shadow crossed Maggie face. "My parents are gone, and even if they weren't..." She paused, staring down at her wine. Her eyes were very wide, very dark when she looked back at him. "Let's just say I never had parents or even grandparents like yours, Jonah."

He didn't want to see the hurt in her eyes. He didn't want to know about her parents. If he knew too much, he'd care too much. So Jonah forced a laugh instead. "Even the best of families have their problems."

"Well, I did notice that your brother wasn't all that keen on either one of us today."

Jonah took another swallow of wine. "Yeah, well, Michael and I aren't getting along too well. What you felt from him today had nothing to do with you."

"Oh?"

"It's business."

"Nothing bad, I hope."

"No, nothing..." Jonah wasn't sure why he paused, and he had no idea why he decided to tell Maggie about the family business troubles. But the shadows in the room grew deeper as he told her how his parents had built the company from nothing.

"I guess Dad was kind of disappointed when I didn't go to work with him," Jonah said as he refilled his wineglass. "Especially since I got an engineering degree. But I never pretended to want to stay, and he never tried to make me feel guilty. Michael was always here. And for the past ten years or so, ever since he graduated from college, he's been right there with Dad."

"So they were very close—Michael and your Dad."

Jonah turned to look at Maggie, frowning. What did she mean by that? "Yeah, sure. Hell, we're a close family. And they worked together, day in, day out. Michael was right there when Dad had his heart attack. Of course they were close. That's why I can't understand what's gotten into Michael."

"What do you mean?"

"He's not doing things the way Dad did them. He's trying to expand too quickly. I mean, Pendleton Construction has always done a certain kind of job—earth-moving projects and light commercial stuff for the most part. Now Michael's bidding on big apartment complexes, hotels." Jonah shook his head. "I'm afraid—no, I'm sure—he's getting in too deep."

Maggie's voice was quiet, even gentle. "Maybe he's just trying to make his mark, you know. Make it his company."

"But it is his," Jonah returned in frustration.

"And you don't want any part of it?"

"Of course not. We always agreed it would be Michael's. He earned it. I didn't."

Maggie wondered if he realized how bitter his words sounded. Maybe the prodigal son, as Michael had called him, really wanted to come home and didn't know how to ask. That possibility appealed to her caretaking instincts and she pressed on, "Michael doesn't want your help or your advice, does he?"

Jonah's laugh was mirthless. "That's an understatement."

"Maybe you're going about it the wrong way." The look he directed at her was sharp, but she continued. "Maybe if he thought you wanted to be a part of the business—"

"But I don't."

"But if you told him you were willing to stay—"

"Wait a minute," Jonah cut in, eyes narrowing. "I'm not willing to stay."

"But if you could stay for, say, six months. If you demonstrated that you really cared—"

"I do really care. I've always cared." Jonah's blue eyes glittered like ice as he set his wineglass down on the floor beside the bottle. "Does the fact that I don't live here all the time automatically exclude me from caring?"

Maggie swallowed, realizing too late that she had intruded on a particularly sensitive subject.

Before she could apologize, Jonah swung his foot to the floor and stood. "I care about my family, Maggie."

"I know. I'm sorry. I just thought—"

"Well, don't think." He turned and started for the door.

Maggie couldn't stand for their day to end on such a sour note. "Jonah, I'm sorry," she said again, as she followed him across the room. He opened the door but turned to face her. For a moment his expression softened, and she stepped closer. Impulsively she placed one hand against his lean cheek. She stroked his unruly hair back from his face. "Jonah, I just wanted to help."

His blue eyes became hard, remote. He shook off her hand. "The best way you can help is by minding your own business."

And though she expected it, Maggie jumped as he slammed the door behind him.

Four

Maggie tapped on the frosted glass door to Liz's office and waited for a response. Receiving none, she turned back to the empty reception area. She had never seen the place so deserted. She could hear voices coming from one of the cubicles on the other side of the room, but no one who sounded like Liz. Perhaps she had gone home on time for once. Maggie turned to leave, wishing she had thought to call before dropping by. Then a chair squeaked on the other side of the door and Maggie opened it slowly, peeking around the edge. "Any hard-working lawyers in here?"

Liz looked up from a cluttered desk, a dazed expression on her face. "Maggie?"

"Last time I checked I was still Maggie, although you don't sound too sure about it. I hope I'm not interrupting anything important. I knocked."

A smile curved Liz's lips as she gestured for her to come inside. "Sorry. I guess I had closed everything out. I'm kind of involved here." With a wave, she indicated the stacks of file folders and thick law books that covered every inch of space in the small, rather dusty cubicle. She started to tuck an errant tendril of chestnut hair into her chignon but ended up removing two of the three pencils she had tucked over her ear. She laughed sheepishly.

Maggie moved a suspiciously aromatic bag from a chair. "Your dinner?"

Liz bit her lip. "Lunch from yesterday. A burrito and beans. I forgot to eat it, unfortunately."

Grimacing, Maggie dropped the bag into an overflowing wastebasket and took a seat. "Looks like you're in the middle of a big case."

"More like the usual backlog of work."

"Then I guess you don't have time to look at any sketches or fabric swatches, do you?"

"Are you kidding?" Liz pushed the files in front of her aside. "I'd love to forget about this mess for a while. What have you got?"

Maggie left her chair and opened a portfolio on top of the cluttered desktop. "If you and Nathan really want to move into the new place before the holidays, you've got to make some decisions."

"I know, I know." Making sounds of approval, Liz flipped through the sketches Maggie had made. Then she started on the wallpaper and fabric swatches, pausing to finger a sample of flowered chintz. "This is exactly what I had in mind for our bedroom. When we find the right furniture—"

"So you didn't find anything you liked at the auction Saturday?" Maggie asked, keeping her voice carefully bland.

"What auct—" A guilty flush crept into Liz's cheeks as she bit back the question. "I mean—"

"It's okay," Maggie retorted. "I know there was no auction. You and Cassandra were about as subtle as jackhammers when you dragged poor Daniel out of my place."

"That bad, huh?" Liz leaned back in her chair. "I'm sorry, Maggie."

"Sure you are."

A teasing light replaced the contrition in Liz's blue eyes. "But it worked out okay, didn't it? Eugenia said you and Jonah went out Sunday. I've been dying to call, but the last few days have been murder. How was it? What did you do?"

Maggie held up a strip of mauve wallpaper. "I was thinking of this for the powder room. What do you—"

"Maggie," Liz warned. "You know I'll get it out of you one way or the other. You might as well surrender now."

"There isn't anything to tell." Maggie tossed the wallpaper sample down and picked up another, scrupulously avoiding her friend's gaze. "I went to dinner at Jonah's grandmother's house."

"An interesting first date."

"Yes, well..." Liz didn't know quite what to say. The day hadn't been exactly a date, but she didn't want to tell Liz that. There was no point in continuing the pretense she and Jonah had agreed upon, but at this point there seemed no reason to go into the whole situation with Liz. Especially since she hadn't seen Jonah in the three days since he had stormed out of her apartment. His car was

gone in the morning when she got up, and though he had
been home every night she didn't have the nerve to go up
to his apartment. She suspected he would prefer that she
stay away and keep her prying little nose out of his business, just as he'd told her.

Liz broke into her thoughts. "Okay, tell me what's
wrong."

"Wrong?"

"You're fiddling with your pearls. A dead giveaway
that something's up."

With an irritated sigh, Maggie let the pearls fall into
place against her rust-colored sweater. "There are times
when I wish my friends didn't know me so well."

"Then something is wrong. With Jonah?"

"Not with him. With me." Maggie curled her fingers
around the cheap fake-leather upholstery of her chair.
Liz wouldn't give up until Maggie told her something. So
finally she blurted, "I think I blew it Sunday." *As if
there was something to blow,* she added silently.

"What did you do?"

"Came on too strong, I guess."

Liz looked at her in surprise. "*You* came on too
strong? Our Maggie—the prude?"

Unexpected anger churned through Maggie. "I'm not
a prude."

"But you always—"

"For God's sake, Liz, sometimes you and Cassandra
both treat me as if I haven't changed one iota since high
school." Maggie gave in to her temper as she got to her
feet. "I have been married, you know. I even had a
child. And I've been dating forever. I'm living in reality,
all right?"

Wide-eyed, Liz was gazing at her as if she was an alien being. "Maggie, I'm sorry. I guess we all think of you—"

"As the fifteen-year-old who wouldn't kiss Frankie Callahan after the ball game," Maggie completed for her, and as quickly as it had come her anger disappeared. "I'm sorry, Liz. I didn't mean to snap at you like that. I don't know what's wrong with me lately."

Liz brushed the apology aside. "There's nothing wrong with you except that you're human. We tend to forget that, Maggie. You've always been so good, so patient."

"Oh, yes, Saint Maggie." Try as she might, Maggie couldn't keep the bitterness from her tone.

"You're not that good," Liz returned in a dry tone. "There was that incident with the stolen cupcakes when we were seven. And that one date with Alex Dalton. He went to second base, and you told me yourself that was one thing you never admitted in confession."

Maggie giggled, remembering, and she and Liz smiled at each other with the ease that can be found only with life-long friends. She sat again, while Liz got up and came around to perch on the edge of the desk.

"So now. Tell me about Jonah."

"It has nothing to do with sex," Maggie began, then blushed, recalling her reactions to Jonah's mere touch, remembering the way he had kissed her.

Liz lifted an eyebrow. "Oh, really?"

"Yes, really. Jonah and I are nothing more than casual acquaintances. At the most we're almost friends. At least I think so. I hope so. But I probably blew it, so it really doesn't matter anyway."

Crossing her arms in her best pensive-lawyer style, Liz slipped off the desk and studied Maggie with a frown.

"If it doesn't matter, why are you babbling like an idiot about him?"

Why was she? Maggie wondered. "Because I think...I mean, I know...I mean..." She swallowed. "I mean, I like him." Even as she said them, the words felt weak and unrepresentative of the feelings Jonah aroused in her.

"Umm." Liz brushed a nonexistent piece of lint from the sleeve of her tailored gray jacket. "*Like* isn't a word I hear much anymore, Maggie. I mean, people do like each other. They're friends. But when a woman talks about a man, she's interested in him, she wants a relat—"

"Okay, okay," Maggie broke in. "Let's not quibble about language, Madame Attorney. Jonah Pendleton is an intriguing man, and even though I shouldn't be interested—"

"Why?"

Maggie shifted in her seat. "Because he's not interested in me."

"You know that for a fact?"

"I'm pretty sure."

"He told you?"

"Would you stop badgering the witness, please?" Maggie slapped her hands against the chair arms. "Just forget I said a word."

"No, Maggie, you can't stop," Liz pleaded. "I promise to behave myself." Accordingly she retreated to her chair and sat, hands folded on the desk in front of her. "Go ahead."

"Great, now you look just like your father, the judge."

"Maggie..."

"All right, all right." Maggie fingered her pearls and took a deep breath. "The thing is, we went out—casually. I got . . . umm . . . shall we say, caught up in the day. I'm attracted to him. We start talking, and I presume too much and stick my nose in where it doesn't belong."

Liz shrugged. "So?"

"So, I blew it."

"Not necessarily."

"Believe me, I did. I was there, remember?"

"So apologize. Make him a batch of your famous banana muffins."

"Jonah isn't the kind of man who can be swayed by homemade food."

A voice from the doorway interrupted them, and Liz's husband stepped into the office. "Well, I am that kind of man, Maggie. Sway me with one of your delicious concoctions."

"Nathan," Liz said. "What are you doing here?"

His hazel eyes dancing with laughter, he leaned across the desk to kiss her. "I was planning to take you to dinner, but if Maggie is cooking—"

"I'm not."

"Oh, please," he wheedled while clearing a stack of papers from another chair. "I know you gave Liz all your best recipes, but . . ." He shrugged, while an indignant Liz scowled at him.

"Why don't you have Maggie give *you* cooking lessons?" she suggested.

"Then what would I tease you about?" Nathan took a seat and regarded both women with his usual charming smile. "If I'm not getting a Maggie-made meal, what lucky guy is? Your new guy, Maggie?"

Maggie gritted her teeth. "I don't have a new guy, and I'm not making muffins or anything else for him."

Nathan frowned. "You're not making muffins for someone who's not your new guy. I'm not sure, but I think there's a contradiction in there somewhere."

"I feel contradictory," Maggie said crossly, then turned to Liz. "As long as Nathan is here, let's look at these sketches and samples."

"Now, Maggie." Liz tapped her desktop to punctuate her words, rather like a teacher scolding a child. "You're just trying to avoid discussing this problem you've got with Jonah. It doesn't sound like a big deal to me, but you have to do something."

"I don't *have* to do anything."

Liz snapped her fingers as if she'd been struck by sudden inspiration. "I know. Bring him to the dinner party Eugenia is having Saturday night."

"Are you crazy?"

"It's a great excuse to ask him out. I know you don't like to do the asking."

Maggie bristled. Why was everyone so sure they knew everything about her?

"I'd opt for the muffins," Nathan suggested. "Take it from a man who knows—Eugenia can be hard on a guy."

"No kidding, Nathan. As if we didn't already know that." Maggie stood and began sifting through her sketches again. "Now if we can just get on with this, please."

"You have to bring someone to Eugenia's," Liz insisted, ignoring her.

"I do not."

"I just hired a new guy in my office. You could bring him," Nathan said.

Liz sent him a withering look. "What are you talking about?"

He spread his hands wide. "Don't look at me like that. I'm just trying to help. Doesn't Maggie need a date?"

"No." Again Maggie gave in to irritation. "Maggie does not need a date." Turning on her heel, she retrieved her purse from the floor and started to leave.

"Now don't go off mad," Liz said.

Nathan got to his feet. "Yeah, don't leave. I was just trying to help."

Maggie paused in the doorway. "You two could help me by looking at those sketches and making some decisions. Every sample is labeled. You've got at least three choices for every room. Please get back to me no later than Friday. Goodbye."

"But what about Jonah?" Liz called.

Maggie didn't stick around to answer.

"A couple of idiots," she muttered to herself as she stalked to the elevator. On the way down to the parking garage, she tried to imagine herself presenting Jonah with a batch of homemade muffins. How silly. Was that the way Liz had dealt with Nathan in the beginning? Hardly. She was much more sophisticated than that. But Liz's suggestion showed just what she thought of Maggie.

"She thinks I'm just a sweet, old-fashioned girl," Maggie whispered, unlocking her car door. "Someone for Nathan to fix up with his new employees." She got in and slammed the door. God, but she was tired of being treated like everyone's poor relation.

Nathan had reminded her of one thing, however. Maggie didn't need a date. She didn't even want a date. Not with anyone they could suggest. Or anyone she knew. Until a certain mustached, blue-eyed imp had caught her attention Friday night, she had been sticking to her vow to forget men for a while. What she had to do was hold fast to that promise. She was going to concentrate on her growing business, on the jobs she had lined up between now and the first of the year. She didn't need romance. She didn't need blue eyes.

She would start anew tonight. Instead of thinking about the man whose apartment was right above hers, she would take a long, hot bath. She would read that book she had started last week. Most of all, she would forget Jonah's smile.

Maggie was still giving herself instructions and making promises an hour later when there was a knock on her back door. Half expecting to find an apologetic Liz and Nathan on her doorstep, she spun it open without even looking.

What she found instead were flowers. A mass of them. Chrysanthemums, mainly. Yellow and bronze. Peeping out from underneath them was a bottle of wine. And two blue-jeaned legs.

The flowers lowered, and the smile she had been trying to forget appeared.

"I know flowers and wine are a bit traditional," Jonah said. "And that's not my usual style." His smile flashed as he handed her the flowers. "Except that these flowers were growing around front. I hope you don't mind."

Maggie laughed. Her insides melted, and all the promises she had made floated into oblivion.

Jonah held out his hand. "Grab a jacket and come with me."

With a jerk and the clang of steel against steel, the construction elevator crept upward. A crisp evening breeze blew through the iron-mesh sides, carrying the smell of plaster and concrete and the stink of exhaust from the cars swishing past on the nearby highway.

Jonah smiled at Maggie. The elevator had only a dim service light, but under the brim of the hard hat he had insisted she wear he could see her eyes were wide and dark. The hat might have robbed some women of their femininity. No one, however, would ever forget Maggie was a woman. Not with her soft-as-moonbeams blond curls. Not with the sweet curves barely hidden under her suede jacket. Jonah had taken to thinking of those curves often in the past few days. Thinking of her body pressed close to his, remembering the way her full breasts had pillowed against his chest.

The elevator creaked, and Jonah came back to the present. He grinned at Maggie's nervous expression. "Were you expecting somewhere a little more finished?"

She nodded and grasped an arm rail as the car shuddered to a halt on the top floor of the partially completed building. "When you said there was somewhere you wanted to take me, I never imagined this place."

"Good. I love surprises. Now stay here for a minute." Jonah slid the elevator's metal doors open and swung his flashlight around until he located the switch for more lights. He turned them on and bowed as Maggie stepped off the elevator. "Welcome, Miss O'Grady, to Pendleton Construction's latest project." His voice echoed off the concrete-and-steel wall as he indicated the debris-strewn, open-sided space with a sweep of his arm. "Might I suggest a table by the window?"

Maggie followed him to the side, but he saw her shudder when he nonchalantly placed the wine bottle on the low concrete wall. "It's a little...*open* up here, isn't it?"

"Scared of heights?" He leaned over to look toward the ground. "It's only six stories. Not too bad."

"I guess that bridge you fell off was higher?"

"Nope. This is probably high enough to kill me."

Maggie shuddered again. "How nice that you can be so matter-of-fact about it."

"To tell the truth, for safety, I'll take a road or a bridge over a building like this any time." He upended two empty plastic buckets. "Your seat, madame."

Still eyeing the edge of the wall nervously, Maggie sat. "Jonah, did you really bring me all the way up here to drink a bottle of wine?"

He produced two plastic cups from his jacket pocket. "Actually, you can only have one glass—cup—of wine. A construction sight is really no place for alcohol, and I'm breaking one of my rules tonight. Safety is the reason you're wearing this." He tapped her hat and handed her the cups.

"So we came up here for a *cup* of wine?"

He sat, pulled a corkscrew from his other pocket and opened the bottle. "The view and the wine are my apology for acting like an ass Sunday night."

"Jonah, that was my fault. I was prying."

He poured wine into both cups. "I invited you to express your opinion, so when you did there was no reason for me to react like an idiot."

"Still—"

"Let's forget it, okay?" He set the wine aside and took a cup from her. "And how about another toast—to our success in pulling the wool over the eyes of our families and friends. You still want to keep up the act, don't you?"

She hesitated but then nodded, and Jonah touched his cup to hers and drank, surprised by the relief he felt.

After his display of temper Sunday evening, he had expected her to slam the door in her face tonight. Maybe if her observations about Michael and the business had been a little less accurate, he wouldn't have gotten so mad. But he shouldn't have taken his anger out on her. He was the one with the guilty conscience.

Not wanting to think about that, Jonah finished his wine and leaned forward. His gaze followed the lighted ribbon of highway below them. Lights from houses and businesses glowed in the darkness, and downtown Nashville's cityscape brightened the horizon. "The view is pretty good, isn't it?"

"When the windows are in, I'm sure it'll be very nice."

He chuckled and glanced at her. "Still nervous, are you?"

"All this talk about safety on the work site hasn't helped." She tugged at the brim of her hat. "I keep expecting something to fall down and hit me in the head."

Jonah stood. "We won't stay around too long if you're that nervous. I just need to check a couple of things."

"So you have to check something, do you? And here I thought you really brought me up here for the view."

"I'll admit I did want a little company."

"You should have waited till tomorrow. I'm sure this place will be swarming with company in the morning."

"But that's just the point . . ." Jonah began, then bit his lip. Dammit, why did this woman have to be so easy to talk to? It was a good thing he wasn't a government official and she wasn't a spy, for he would have spilled all his secrets in no time.

Maggie set her cup down and said nothing, although she had a hundred questions. Why was Jonah poking around one of his brother's job sites after hours? Was there something wrong with the construction? Nervously she gazed at the concrete and steel above her. She clutched the brim of her hat again and scrambled to her feet.

"You stay here," Jonah told her, turning to walk away.

"Nothing doing. I'm going with you." Stuffing the cork back into the wine bottle, she hurried after him.

Nervousness of a different nature set in, however, when he took her hand in his. His hand was just as she had remembered it—broad, hard and unmistakably male. She wondered, as she had several times during the past few days, what those hands would feel like on her skin. He would know how to touch a woman, Maggie decided. He would know just where to linger. Her nipples tightened at his imagined caress. Her heart began an erratic rhythm. She was so wrapped up in her fantasy, she stumbled against a stack of concrete blocks.

"You okay?" Jonah asked, catching her.

"Yes, fine." Maggie dropped his hand and rubbed her shin. In the interest of safety, Maggie didn't take his hand again. Even his simplest touch was too dangerous.

He looked around the top floor and did the same on the one below. Maggie couldn't imagine what he had discovered just by looking, but by the time they got on the elevator to go down the fourth floor his mouth was set in a grim line. She had all she could do just to keep from asking him what was wrong.

Then the elevator jerked to a halt.

"What's wrong?" Maggie demanded.

Frowning, Jonah pushed the controls. Nothing happened. "We'll give it a minute. It'll probably start right back up. These things can get cantankerous from time to time."

"Why doesn't that reassure me?" She edged away from the metal-mesh side. Jonah had the nerve to chuckle, and she glared at him. "It's not funny. What if we're trapped here all night?"

"Don't worry. We could climb out if we had to. We haven't even cleared the fifth floor yet." He pointed upward. Beyond the metal-mesh doors the concrete edge of the floor they had just left was within reach. In front of them was concrete, supported by a steel girder. Below that was a narrow opening that indicated the beginning of the fourth floor. "We might even be able to squeeze out down here."

"Then let's do it."

"I'm sure this thing will start moving in a couple of minutes."

Maggie turned back to the view. It was too dark to see anything clearly, but the ground looked very far away. She shivered, thinking how it might feel to plunge four and a half stories. This cage they were in would probably collapse on them like a set of giant metal teeth.

She whirled back to face Jonah. "Does this have anything to do with what you were looking for?"

He shook his head and again pushed the controls. The elevator didn't respond.

"I was kind of surprised to see an elevator here in the first place," Maggie continued, preferring her voice to the silence. "I thought they were strictly for skyscrapers."

"You'll see them nowadays on lots of jobs of more than four stories. When they're working they save a lot of time." He pressed the unresponsive controls again and grimaced. "And my brother needs to save all the time he can."

Her questions rushed out before she could think about whether she was prying. "Is that why you're poking around here tonight? Has Michael cut corners to save time?"

Jonah leaned against the side of the car. "No, he hasn't cut corners." After rummaging in his jacket he withdrew a cigar like the one he had smoked Sunday. His lighter flashed, and the cigar tip glowed as he inhaled.

Maggie's impatience got the better of her. "If he hasn't cut corners, why are you here?"

"Because I wanted to see for myself what I suspected," Jonah retorted, sounding like a man who had given up trying to hide anything. "He's probably two months behind on the job."

"Is that a lot?"

"It is, considering he's that much and more behind on every other project the company has going."

"But construction delays are unavoidable. I've decorated many places that were weeks or months behind schedule. I know how things can be held up by the weather, by suppliers, by—"

"Yeah, but the way my brother is operating is a good way to ruin the firm's reputation."

"Surely a little run of bad luck won't do too much harm."

"It wouldn't be a disaster if Michael hadn't also underbid three of the current projects. Right now the company is losing money in a big way, even though he has twice as many jobs as he can handle." Jonah had no idea why he was telling Maggie about his worries. The woman just had a way of making him talk.

"What does Michael have to say about all of this?" she asked quietly.

"To me he says as little as possible." Jonah fixed his gaze on the faraway traffic and took a deep drag on his cigar. Then, with an impatient muttered oath, he crushed it out on the side of the elevator. "Why am I smoking? I had given up these damn things before I came back here."

"So Michael has driven you to smoke, has he?"

Maggie's amused voice cleared some of Jonah's impatience. He grinned at her. "That little brother of mine is probably going to drive me to worse than that before it's all over."

"But what can you do?"

"I can hope he'll let me help him. Hell, I don't pretend to be an expert at what he's doing. I build roads and bridges, not office buildings. But I could do more if he'd let me. I could help him coordinate things, get more done in less time. But no—all he has me doing is overseeing a parking-lot project. And I bet I wouldn't be doing that if Mom didn't still have a say in the business."

He searched his jacket for a new cigar, then swore, apparently remembering he had quit. "The least Michael could do is talk to me. I've had to question Mom and sneak around to find out what I have. I'm here at ten o'clock on a Wednesday night so that no one will see me and report it back to Michael. He resents me even asking questions."

"He feels threatened? Thinks you want to take the company away from him?"

Jonah considered that for a moment and then sighed. "Actually I believe it has more to do with what you suggested the other night. If I told Michael I wanted part of the business, that I was going to stay around, he'd probably be willing to let me help.''

''Maybe he doesn't want to get himself in a position of depending on you.''

She could certainly cut to the heart of an issue, Jonah decided as guilt started its habitual squeeze on his chest. This time instead of growing angry he just turned away from her, muttering, ''Yeah, well, depending on me is the worst thing anybody could do.''

Maggie crossed the elevator to his side. ''You took what I said a little differently than I meant it.''

He shrugged. ''Michael's probably wise not to listen to me or include me in any decisions. After all, I'm going to leave in a few months, just the way I left twelve years ago.''

''Would you rather stay here and run the business?''

''No, but...'' Jonah shoved his hands in his jacket pockets. Explaining how he felt was just too hard. ''Maybe I should just leave now. Mom can call me with the news when the company goes bankrupt.''

''You don't mean that.''

''I know.'' He kicked against the elevator side. ''It's just so damn frustrating, watching him ruin Dad's business.''

''*Dad's?*''

Jonah held up a hand. ''I know, I know, it's Michael's business now, but if he loses it...'' He sucked in his breath. ''If I let him lose it—''

''You can't assume that responsibility.''

''But I have, you know. In my mind if Michael messes up, then I will have let Dad down.'' He looked out at the night and whispered. ''Let him down again.''

''Why do you say again?''

"Because if I had stayed here, if I had helped . . ." Jonah shook his head. He had never put those thoughts into words before.

"But you told me Sunday night that your father wasn't upset when you didn't come to work with him."

"He was that way. If Michael and I had both decided to join the circus, he probably would have cheered us on."

Maggie's voice was soft. "He sounds like a great father."

"The best." Jonah gripped the cool metal of the elevator's arm rail, wishing he had his emotions as firmly in hand. "Sometimes I wish Dad had asked me to stay. I probably would have."

"Would you have been happy with that?"

"No," he admitted reluctantly. "I would have hated it. At least for a while. But maybe with me *and* Michael beside him, Dad wouldn't have worked so hard these past few years. He could have slowed down and taken care of himself. And maybe he wouldn't have died." He let his shoulders slump as he considered what might have been.

His remorseful stance touched Maggie's heart. Without giving much thought to her actions, she slipped her arm through his and pressed her cheek against his shoulder. She knew something about regrets, about the what-ifs and possibilities that could haunt you for years. She didn't like to see Jonah torturing himself that way. "You can't change what happened to your father. It isn't your fault," she whispered.

"Those are just words, Maggie. They're sometimes hard to believe."

"What you do is repeat them over and over. Until one day you'll realize they're true."

"Are you speaking from experience?"

"Yeah, I am." Maggie stepped away from him and folded her arms against her chest. She shivered in the suddenly cold breeze. "I had rotten parents, Jonah. They fought all the time. My father gambled away every dime he had or could make or could wheedle out of my grandfather. My mother was an alcoholic. She took all her anger and her frustration out on Daniel. Sometimes with her fist. Sometimes with the things, *horrible things* she would say." Maggie closed her eyes. Jonah was right. There were some wounds that never stopped bleeding.

He laid a comforting hand on her shoulder and she looked up into blue eyes shadowed with sympathy. "I'm sorry, Maggie."

She managed a smile and continued, "Thanks, but like I said, Daniel suffered more than I did. And somehow I was able to put things in perspective better than he. I spent a lot of time at my grandparents' house. My grandfather wasn't the greatest, but when I was there I spent time with Liz and Cassandra who lived down the street." Maggie paused. "And then there was Eugenia."

"You said she was like a mother to you."

Maggie nodded. "Underneath all her eccentric ways she's one very smart lady, and she taught me a lot. One day when my parents had done something—I don't remember what—I sat next to Eugenia and cried and told her all the things I wished I could change about my life. I was about twelve, so you can imagine that I had a whole list of problems."

"It's a rotten age."

"Yes, but Eugenia told me something that day that I've never forgotten. She said that everyone's life is like a bunch of balloons. Some of the balloons pop. Others drift away. Others just deflate. It's inevitable, and you can't change it. And if you spend all your time worrying about the balloons that disappear, you'll never enjoy the ones that remain."

Jonah sighed and rubbed his fingers across his mustache. "It's a nice story, but—"

"Stop agonizing over what you can't change, Jonah."

"But if I have a chance to make it right? What then?"

"The moral of the story is that you can't make it right," Maggie told him, irritated because he seemed to have missed the point. "You can't change the past. You can't stay here and help Michael in order to make up for the years you weren't here. The only way you'll do him any good is if you decide to stay because it's what *you* want."

"But it isn't." The words burst from Jonah before he gave them any thought. But they were true. He couldn't imagine staying here for more than a few months at most. For the first time in his life he wished he didn't have this need, this hunger to be on the move. He wished it would be enough to settle down in one place, to love someone like Maggie...

That thought brought him up short. Settling down with anyone was the last thing he wanted. He glanced sharply at Maggie, at her sweet, concerned expression, her kissable mouth. She was the sort of woman who could unfurl her soft, perfumed net faster than most men could think. He had spent his life avoiding nets. But maybe his luck was running out.

The elevator was suddenly very small.

"What are we doing standing around like this is some cocktail party? Let's get out of here." He hit the controls again. Again there was no movement, so he pushed open the mesh door that faced the building. The edge of the fifth floor was just above eye level, and there was plenty of space between the floor and the top of the elevator. A piece of cake, he decided.

He found a foothold in one side of the door. "I'm going to climb up. Then I'll help you."

"Why can't we go down?" Maggie pointed to the narrow opening at the bottom of the elevator.

"Because I don't relish landing on this leg of mine."

"Won't you hurt it climbing up, too?"

"Fortunately this requires more upper-body strength." He lifted his hands to the concrete floor and pushed up with his good leg. With very little strain, he scrambled onto the concrete floor. His legs swung over the edge as he sat up and grinned down at Maggie. "No sweat. I didn't even lose my hat."

"A fat lot of good these hats have done us tonight." Grasping the hand he offered for leverage, Maggie began climbing up, too. She had her torso over the floor's edge when she said, "Shouldn't I bring the wine?"

"Just leave—"

The elevator sprang to life then, obliterating Jonah's voice. He had only seconds to jerk Maggie onto the floor and swing his legs out of the way of the moving car. A stinging pain shot up his right leg as they rolled clear, and they ended up with Maggie half pinned to the floor beneath him. He hugged her close, for a moment gripped by the terrifying vision of her body wedged between the elevator and the building.

Forgetting everything but his relief, he pressed his face against her neck. "Oh, God, Maggie, I'm sorry. I forgot to press the lever that would keep it from moving. God, I'm sorry. I almost got us killed."

"It's okay. I'm all right . . ."

The wild hammering of her heart beneath his fingers belied her words, and that was when Jonah realized one of his hands rested against the gentle swell of her breast. He knew a sensible man, a man who avoided nets, would pull away. But he didn't. Instead he cupped her breast and brushed his lips across the pulse beating in her throat. Her skin was soft. He sweet fragrance filled his head. And his body stirred in reaction.

For a moment he was lost, only aware of how close she was and how hard he had become. Then he shook himself mentally. What was he doing? They could have been hurt, and here he was behaving like a randy teenager at a touch-football game. He was actually *copping a feel*! He sat up and groaned, half because his leg throbbed in pain, half because he would rather follow his adolescent urges and stay tangled on the floor with Maggie.

"Are you all right?" she asked, sitting up also.

Except for the usual safety lights, it was dim on this floor, so he couldn't tell by her expression whether she had been aware of what he had done. Maybe she hadn't. Maybe in the tension and relief of the moment... Oh, hell, he thought. It didn't really matter. The important thing was that they get out of this building. He had to get away from her before he backed her up against a steel girder and kissed her pretty pink mouth and lost himself in her gently rounded curves.

He reached for the flashlight that had rolled out of his pocket and offered her a hand up. "Are you okay?" he demanded, his voice gruffer than he had intended.

"Yeah, I'm fine, but you—"

"Let's just go home." Without pausing, he turned and started for the opening where the stairs should be located.

"Wait a minute," Maggie said. "We're forgetting our hats." She picked them up from the floor.

Jonah's suggestion for what they should do to the hats was quick and to the point. But he took his and rammed it on his head anyway and proceeded toward the stairs again.

Maggie followed, noticing that his limp was more pronounced and wondered if her friends would ever believe how she had spent this evening. Climbing out of elevators was a far cry from baking banana muffins.

It wasn't until after Jonah had brought her home, long after she had slipped into a steaming tub of water, that Maggie allowed herself to think of that moment they had lain together on that cold concrete floor. Had she imagined the touch of his hand? The whisper of his lips against her skin? Surely she hadn't invented the way his body had tightened.

Sliding deeper into the cooling water in her tub, Maggie thought through the moment with Jonah again. And again. And still once more.

Later she wasn't sure if it was the hour in the tub or the thoughts of Jonah that had turned her legs to spaghetti. But she was certain who had caused the deep, yearning ache in the pit of her stomach.

Five

Fine crystal and silver glinted in the candlelight. The air was scented by flowers. In the background a piano tinkled softly, the perfect accompaniment to the low murmur of conversation. The surroundings bespoke elegance and old money. The wine was vintage. The veal superb.

Yet Jonah wished for a beer and a burger.

He gazed down Eugenia's long dining-room table at Maggie, who sat talking with the man on her left. Just watching her made Jonah correct his wish. What he really wanted was a beer, a burger and her.

They should leave, he thought. They should find some hole-in-the-wall dive on Printer's Alley. Where the bartender's name was Mac. And the jukebox played slow songs. They should do some swaying on a smoky dance floor. His leg could stand the strain if they moved real slow. And slow was the only way he wanted to move with

Maggie. He could put his arms around her and settle his chin against the smooth, white skin of her shoulder. He could kiss her there. And on her sweet, sweet mouth. While they were dancing he'd have an excuse to put his hands all over her. Run them down her sides. From the curve of her breasts to her saucy, swaying hips.

"Don't you care for veal?"

The question penetrated the imaginary scene Jonah had been setting. With reluctance, he pulled his gaze from Maggie and looked at Eugenia. She sat at the head of her table, reigning over her dinner party, resplendent in an emerald satin dress. He was seated closest to her on one side of the table. Those sharp blue eyes of hers made him think she knew exactly where his mind had been.

The diamonds on her fingers flashed as she picked up her goblet of wine. "Not a fan of veal?" she repeated.

"Actually it's wonderful, but..." Jonah allowed his gaze to stray back to Maggie, at the other end of the table. He smiled. "I guess I'm preoccupied."

Eugenia chuckled. "And I guess I'll forgive you for that."

"I'm sure you're pleased with my preoccupation."

Her laughter deepened. "I believe you're a bit of a cad, Jonah Pendleton."

"I've been called worse."

"A cad with a touch of wanderlust in your soul."

He nodded. "I'm impressed. You seem to have me pretty well pegged."

"You're not so hard to read. Especially since I asked Daniel and Maggie to tell me all about you."

"And here I thought you were psychic."

The humor in her blue eyes came and went quickly and she leaned forward, her voice dropping to a whisper. "You're not planning on breaking her heart, are you?"

She was nothing if not blunt, Jonah decided as he touched a fine linen napkin to his lips. He wanted to tell Eugenia she needn't fear what he would do to Maggie's heart. He had no plans for Maggie.

Or did he?

If he had no plans, why had he been fantasizing about dancing with her, touching her? For a man who was supposed to be *pretending* an attraction to her, his response to her was all too real. And if he were honest with himself, he would admit he had felt this way from the first moment they had looked at each other. He wanted to resist Maggie, to think of her as a friend, a landlady, Daniel O'Grady's sister. But she was a woman. And everything about her reminded him he was a man. Especially when she wore dresses like the one she had on tonight. All black and shimmery. With her shoulders and half her bosom bare.

"Well?" Eugenia's delicate eyebrows rose a bit. "Are you going to hurt her?"

Jonah cleared his throat, wishing he was as sure of his answer as he had been a week ago. It was ironic, really. "Eugenia, shouldn't you have worried about that before you so . . . *subtly* pushed us together?"

"It looks to me as if you didn't need much pushing."

He glanced back at Maggie. Eugenia was right. His own desire had pushed him toward Maggie. His own, highly inappropriate desire. For Maggie wasn't a woman who would let a man walk away easily, and walking away was what Jonah did best. "I'd never want to hurt her," he told Eugenia softly.

"I'll hold you to those words."

Jonah imagined she would do just that. There was plenty of fight left in this woman, and she had the look of someone who would defend those she loved.

"I'm protective of my girls," she murmured, echoing his thoughts.

"Maggie has told me how close all of you are."

"Yes." Her expression softened. "Liz and Maggie and Cassandra are my treasures."

Jonah followed her gaze down the table to the three women. Just looking at them told him how different each was from the other. There was Liz of the classically perfect features and the sapphire eyes. Cool sophistication clung to her as well as her ivory gown draped her slender figure. Cassandra was the other side of the coin. Her flashing dark eyes and curling, ebony hair matched her uninhibited laughter and her outrageously revealing scarlet dress. And Maggie? Maggie anchored the other two with her warmth. There was something soothing about her steady brown eyes, something unconsciously sexy about the way she moved, the way she smiled.

"I'd say you're lucky," Jonah said, his gaze remaining on Maggie as he spoke to Eugenia. "Your treasures are rare indeed."

Eugenia laughed. "You're an astute man, Jonah." She proceeded to tell him how, when Liz, Cassandra and Maggie were eighteen, she had given them each a favorite piece of her jewelry. More symbolic than merely valuable, the gifts reflected the girls' personalities. Diamond earrings for brilliant Liz. A ruby ring for fiery Cassandra. "And the pearls for Maggie. Because she hides her heart, just as an oyster hides its prize."

So the pearls had been Eugenia's, Jonah thought. Their creamy luster suited Maggie's mellow kind of beauty. Eugenia had made the right choice, and as she said, Maggie's heart would be a prize for the right man. The search for that heart might be an interesting journey.

But only for the right man.

And dammit, that wasn't him.

If I just hadn't kissed her, he chastised himself. If only he hadn't followed that stupid, reckless impulse, he wouldn't know anything about this woman's passionate depths. And this growing attraction to her would be easier to fight. But he had kissed her. He knew how she could respond. That was why he had pawed at her like some schoolboy the other night. That was why he sat here now, surrounded by Eugenia's guests, wondering just what Miss Maggie O'Grady was wearing under that clingy, shimmering dress of hers.

Eugenia's laugh was soft in his ear, forcing Jonah to realize how hard he was clutching the stem of his wine goblet. She touched the sleeve of his jacket. "I hope you don't disappoint me, Jonah Pendleton."

He let out a long-held breath and forced himself to smile. "So do I, Eugenia. So do I."

As Eugenia's husky laughter trickled down the table, Maggie looked up with a frown. Jonah's head was bent close to the older woman's. What was she telling him? She had monopolized his attention all evening. Maggie suffered through the dessert course and headed toward Jonah as soon as everyone began moving toward the parlor for after-dinner drinks and coffee.

Cassandra, however, intercepted her. "Don't look so worried," she whispered.

"I'm not worried."

"Yes, you are. I can always tell."

Maggie realized she was fiddling with her pearls and flushed. What did Cassandra and Liz do, anyway, sit around and compare notes on her idiosyncrasies and bad habits?

"You have nothing to worry about," Cassandra continued. "Jonah was sneaking looks at you all during dinner. I told you this dress would do the trick."

Resisting the urge to tug at her plunging neckline, Maggie nodded. This dress had been Liz and Cassandra's idea. She knew it was flattering, but it wasn't her usual style. All night she had felt as if every man she talked with had looked first at her breasts. However, there had been that moment when Jonah had first seen her. His clear blue eyes had darkened. He had smiled his lazy smile of approval. He liked the way she looked, and perhaps that knowledge made the dress perfect.

Maggie told herself his opinion shouldn't matter. She had known the man only a week, and already she was courting his approval. She watched for his car in the evening. She listened for his step on the stairs. For the past two nights they had sat on her back porch, enjoying the unseasonably mild weather, drinking coffee and talking. Their chats had been nothing more than friendly, but Maggie's stomach had done strange flip-flops whenever he so much as looked at her. Tonight had been no better. She definitely had a problem.

Morosely she watched as he tucked Eugenia's hand in the crook of his elbow and prepared to escort her from the dining room. His gaze met Maggie's first, however, and the wink he sent her way was playful. The smile he gave her was intimate, as if they shared some sexy secret.

Their only secret was this hoax they were carrying out, but Maggie's stomach started its familiar flutter anyway. Eugenia beamed in her direction as they left.

Cassandra drew in her breath. "Well, Maggie, I'll say one thing for him. He's a definite charmer."

Charming and footloose and absolutely wrong for me, Maggie thought. Yet she stood rooted to the spot, staring at the doorway through which he had disappeared while the rest of the dinner guests vacated the room.

Cassandra giggled. "You've got it bad, haven't you?"

Maggie tried to hide her reaction to Jonah with a smile. But she couldn't, and she knew Cassandra was off to make a report to Liz and Eugenia when she left the dining room. Maggie lingered in the dining room, moving to the side as two maids began clearing the table. How was she going to resist Jonah?

She was so caught in her thoughts she jumped when someone touched her shoulder. She whirled around to find Jeannette, Eugenia's French maid and cook, surveying her with shrewd brown eyes.

"You come with me, *chérie*," Jeannette ordered.

Maggie didn't consider disobeying. Jeannette's black uniform crackled with starch as she led the way to the kitchen.

For forty years Jeannette had served Eugenia faithfully, becoming more than an employee. Eugenia and Liz and Liz's parents regarded her as one of the family, and she could have retired from her duties. Yet she continued to work hard, supervising a staff of two and cooking most of the meals, especially those for the dinner parties Eugenia loved to throw. Liz, Maggie and Cassandra had bedeviled her when they were children—stealing the cookies she made for Eugenia's famous teas and hiding the romantic novels she devoured like candy.

Her loyalty to Eugenia had earned her their respect. Her sweetness and generosity had earned her their love.

In the kitchen, Jeannette poured aromatic black coffee, added ample portions of sugar and cream and pressed the cup into Maggie's hands before she could protest.

"Drink up and tell me your troubles." Twenty years in America hadn't robbed Jeannette of her accent. She bustled across the room to the dishwasher, asking over her shoulder, "It is the rogue who causes you to frown, yes?"

"The rogue?"

"His name is Jonah, is it not?"

Maggie nodded. She should have guessed Jeannette would know about Jonah. Nothing and no one who entered this house escaped her notice for long. And there was Eugenia, of course. Everything Eugenia knew was passed on to Jeannette, and Eugenia had pumped Maggie for information about Jonah on the phone yesterday. She wouldn't be surprised if Eugenia had put a private investigator on his tail. "You think he's a rogue?" Maggie asked Jeannette.

"He has that look about him. The too long hair. The blue eyes and mustache. The limp. His is enough to make a mademoiselle's heart flutter, no?"

"Yes." Maggie sighed and sipped her rich, sweet coffee. "That's exactly what he does."

"You think he is what . . . dangerous?"

"Very."

"Exciting?"

Again Maggie sighed, closing her eyes, trying to fight the memory of Jonah's hand on her breast. "Absolutely, positively exciting."

PLAY THE
LUCKY CARNIVAL WHEEL

scratch-off game
and get as many as
SIX FREE GIFTS...

HOW TO PLAY:

1. With a coin, carefully scratch off the silver area at right. Then check your number against the chart below it to find out which gifts you're eligible to receive.

2. You'll receive brand-new Silhouette Desire® novels and possibly other gifts—ABSOLUTELY FREE! Send back this card and we'll promptly send you the free books and gifts you qualify for!

3. We're betting you'll want more of these heartwarming romances, so unless you tell us otherwise, every month we'll send you 6 more wonderful novels to read and enjoy. Always delivered right to your home. And always at a discount off the cover price!

4. Your satisfaction is guaranteed! You may return any shipment of books and cancel at any time. The Free Books and Gifts remain yours to keep!

NO COST! NO RISK!
NO OBLIGATION TO BUY!

More Good News For Members Only!

When you join the Silhouette Reader Service™, you'll receive 6 heartwarming romance novels each month delivered to your home. You'll also get additional free gifts from time to time as well as our members-only newsletter. It's your privileged look at upcoming books and profiles of our most popular authors!

If offer card is missing, write to: Harlequin Reader Service, 901 Fuhrmann Blvd., P.O. Box 1867, Buffalo, NY 14269-1867

MAIL THIS CARD TODAY!

BUSINESS REPLY CARD

First Class   Permit No. 717   Buffalo, NY

Postage will be paid by addressee

SILHOUETTE
READER SERVICE
901 FUHRMANN BLVD
PO BOX 1867
BUFFALO NY 14240-9952

NO POSTAGE
NECESSARY
IF MAILED
IN THE
UNITED STATES

Jeannette laughed heartily, her plump cheeks growing rosier than usual. "This is good, Maggie. A little danger. A little excitement. This is what a woman needs from a man."

"You've read one too many books," Maggie retorted. She had read many of the same books, since she was as fond of love stories as Jeannette. She had, however, never taken them seriously, and her expectations of what she should look for in a man had stayed firmly rooted in practicality, "I like men who are settled and secure."

Jeannette sniffed. "I have seen you with a dozen men like that. Not one makes you sigh as this Jonah does."

"But he isn't really interested in me. He's leaving—"

"What men say they will do and what they do...oh, *chérie*, those are different things."

"But—"

Jeannette took the coffee cup out of Maggie's hand and shooed her toward the door. "Now go to him. Flutter your eyelashes. Show yourself off in your pretty dress."

Turning to leave, Maggie looked down and pressed a hand to the cleavage revealed by her dress. "I think I'm showing off a little more than necessary tonight," she said ruefully. "Tell me honestly, Jeannette, is it too much?"

"No."

The answer didn't come from Jeannette, and Maggie jerked her head up. Jonah leaned against the doorjamb, his arms crossed, a hint of mystery in his smile. In his conservative dark suit, he looked every bit as male, every bit as dangerous as he had appeared in his leather jacket and T-shirt. Dangerous and excitingly male, just as she had told Jeannette he was.

Maggie's cheeks grew warm as she stared at him. At her breast, her hand clenched into a fist. She held it that way until she realized how silly she must look. Jonah's smile only deepened as her arm fell to her side.

"The dress is just right," he said. His gaze moved over her like a caress. Her breasts tightened in response, and an ache started deep in her stomach.

Yet Maggie finally found her voice. "What . . . what are you doing in here?"

"I wondered where you were. Eugenia said you might be back here."

"I was talking to Jeannette." Maggie turned to the Frenchwoman, whose face was wreathed in a smile. Quickly Maggie performed the introductions, explaining how important Jeannette was to Eugenia and to her. "Jeannette taught me to cook," she said. "I spent a lot of time in this kitchen."

"Perhaps Maggie should make one of her special dinners for you, Monsieur Pendleton," Jeannette suggested coyly. Maggie wanted to kick her.

Jonah's mustache twitched slightly. "Perhaps she should. What would you say is her specialty, Jeannette?" But before the woman could answer, the two maids arrived with a service cart loaded with crystal and china.

"We should get back to the party," Maggie said hastily. With a last furious glance at Jeannette, she led the way down the hall. They needed to get back to the safety of numbers. They needed other people to diffuse the awareness between them.

Jonah took her elbow as they started down the hallway from the kitchen. It was a big house and a long hall and he walked intentionally slowly, in no hurry to rejoin the others. Not that the company wasn't enjoyable.

Eugenia was an interesting woman, not at all the boring society matron he had pegged her as in the beginning. Daniel was a good guy, and Jonah enjoyed talking to Cassandra, Liz and Nathan. And he was intrigued by Herbert Black, the courtly millionaire who hung on Eugenia's every word. The country-music video producer, the state senator and the other guests weren't exactly dull, either. Liz had told him Eugenia liked assembling diverse groups of people and then sitting back to enjoy their interaction.

Jonah, however, had found himself looking around for Maggie, thinking about the past few evenings when they had sat on her back porch and talked. He had realized that despite the lively conversation in Eugenia's living room, he would prefer to be with Maggie. And Maggie alone.

Just a half hour ago he had attributed his feelings about her to the way she filled out her dress, which proved he could be as superficial as the next guy when it came to a woman's more obvious assets. But he had realized something else while he had stood in Eugenia's living room, wondering where Maggie had gone. The way he was beginning to feel about her went much deeper than an appreciation of her breasts or hips or legs. He just enjoyed being with her. It didn't matter whether they were discussing the merits of coffee beans over prepackaged-grind or the state of the federal debt. She listened. She had thoughtful, sensible things to say. She made him feel good. Damn good. Better than any woman had ever made him feel.

Ignoring the caution signals that were going off in his head, he pulled her into the next room they passed.

"Jonah, what—"

"Humor me, all right? I've had enough party chit-chat for a while." He paused just inside the door and whistled appreciatively. "Man, this is a great room."

Floor-to-ceiling bookshelves covered two walls. In front of the three long windows was a desk. A couple of chairs with comfortable-looking tweed-upholstered cushions were arranged in front of a small fireplace. Underfoot was a thick Oriental rug in shades of green and gold.

"The perfect place for a good read on a stormy night," Jonah murmured, reaching out to touch the smooth leather bindings of a row of books.

Maggie switched on the green-shaded banker's lamp on the desk. "That's exactly how I intended the room to look."

He sent another admiring glance around, noting the graceful wooden sculpture on a pedestal near the desk, the careful arrangement of framed certificates on the wall between the windows. "It's impressive, Maggie. Very much so."

"Liz's father uses this as his study when he's home. He wanted it redone last year."

"I thought this was Eugenia's house."

"It's the family's home. Eugenia's grandfather built it. It passed to his son and then to Liz's mother. Eventually I'm sure Liz and Nathan and their children will live here."

"And are Liz's parents hiding somewhere tonight?"

"They're in Mexico, I think. He's a retired judge. They travel a lot."

Jonah turned slowly in the center of the room. "This looks like a judge's room. Very dignified. Yet comfortable."

"I'll tell him you approve," Maggie retorted, coming to stand beside him.

The painting over the mantel drew Jonah's attention. "It's Eugenia, isn't it?"

"About fifty years ago. Doesn't Liz resemble her?"

He nodded. Eugenia had been lovely. A smile tilting her lips. Blue eyes shining. Around her neck were the pearls Maggie now wore. "Your necklace, right?" he asked, turning to her.

"I see Eugenia has been telling you stories."

"The pearls suit you."

"Thank you." She touched the necklace lovingly.

Because Jonah suddenly wanted to touch her the same way, he shoved his hands in his pockets and turned back to Eugenia's portrait. "She looks like a bride here. Was she?"

Maggie laughed. "Almost." At his questioning glance, she went on to explain. "Eugenia was engaged. Her fiancé gave her these pearls. She had her wedding dress designed and wore it for this portrait. She even ordered invitations. And then she ran away."

"Somehow that sounds like her. But why?"

"I'm not really sure," Maggie said slowly, her eyes growing dreamy. "She's never gone into all the details, but I know the man was an Englishman, a journalist who became a fighter pilot in the War. The Germans shot him down a few years later."

"And Eugenia? Who did she marry?"

"No one."

Jonah was surprised. "But she's such a fan of marriage."

"Not marriage, in particular," Maggie pointed out. "Just the part about pairing off."

"Kind of makes you wonder why she ran away from her pilot, doesn't it?"

"Every Sunday and most days during the week she has tea, a habit she says he instilled in her." Again Maggie fingered her necklace. "And she kept his pearls."

"She watched you wear them on your wedding day, didn't she?"

He could see his question startled her, but Jonah had been wondering about this ex-husband of hers. What sort of man would let go of Maggie O'Grady? She was a woman who had been born to be a wife. Any fool could see that.

"I wore them," she answered slowly. "But Eugenia boycotted the ceremony."

"Why would she do that?"

"Because she said I was too young to get married. And she was right. As usual." Maggie's smile was sad, her tone accepting.

"So that was the reason for the divorce. You were too young?"

"Too young. Too foolish. Barry—"

"Your husband?"

"Yes. Barry Lewis. I was nineteen. We were both in school. We had no money. We had to live with my mother. By that point my father had gone for good, and Mother was drinking heavily. Barry and I should have waited, but..." Maggie sighed, then shook her head. "Oh, well, it's all ancient history now. I'm sure you don't care—"

"Sure I do."

Maggie's gaze flashed up to meet his. She frowned.

"You couldn't have been married long," Jonah said quickly, before she could ask him why he cared. It was a question for which he didn't have an answer.

"Barry and I were married two years." Maggie bit her bottom lip, and there was regret in her voice. "It was long enough to hurt each other."

He felt compelled to take her hand, offer her some comfort. "I can't see you hurting anyone, Maggie. Least of all someone you loved. I know you had to have loved him, or you wouldn't have married him."

"You would think so, wouldn't you?" Her laugh was hollow, and she slipped her hand from his. "Right now, all I know is that I loved the thought of marrying him and the idea of having a family. A good family. I think I wanted to prove I could succeed where my parents had failed."

He could understand that, considering what she had told him about her parents the other night. After growing up in the midst of chaos, she had wanted something different for herself. "Even though you were young, there had to have been something specific that went wrong about the marriage."

Maggie shrugged, but there was nothing nonchalant about her voice as she answered. "Mother died. Barry flunked out of school. We had…" She paused, her gaze skipped back to Jonah's for a moment. He wondered what she had left out as she rushed on. "We had arguments. He realized he was missing part of life by being married and having to deal with so many problems. I tried to change him. And he left." There was a trace, however small, of defeat in her words.

And for a moment Jonah felt a sharp, burning fury at the man who had hurt her. With a light touch, he raised her chin and tilted her face toward his. "I'll give you ten-to-one that he regrets losing you now."

A smile chased the pensive shadows from her brown eyes. "You're good for the ego, Mr. Pendleton."

With careful deliberation, Jonah surrendered to the impulse he had been fighting and touched a finger to her pearls. They were warm from her skin. As creamy as her skin. But not nearly as soft. His finger glided slowly from pearl to pearl. Then under the pearls, across her skin. Had anything ever felt this soft?

Maggie's hand caught his. Finally. Before he reached the dusky shadow between her breasts. "Jonah."

He looked at her as if he was in a dream. He blinked, then smiled a slumberous smile while his attention seemed focused on her lips. The hand she didn't hold brushed through her hair. He looked as if he would kiss her. Already she could taste him against her mouth, though he hadn't moved.

But instead of kissing her, he just looked at her. And perhaps that was more intimate than a kiss, Maggie decided later. Because while she waited for him to make a move, she had time to anticipate the moist glide of his tongue against her lips. She imagined the satisfied sound he would make deep in his throat. The way her heart would pound. The heat in his gaze when they drew apart.

The heat was the one thing she didn't imagine, because when Jonah finally did release her, the very air between them was smoldering. Even if he really had kissed her, Maggie couldn't imagine that she could feel any more aroused.

And she knew Jonah felt the same way.

Yet he didn't say a word. Neither did she. He just took her by the hand and led her back to the party. Then he didn't touch her again. Not even casually. Not that night.

Or the next day.

Or all the next week.

They saw each other, however. Every night Jonah came down for coffee and a chat. When a cold front moved in, they switched from her porch to her kitchen. He built a fire in the fireplace. She used one of Jeannette's best recipes to make him some cookies. He told her about putting highways through deserts and bridges over swamps. There was wonder in his voice as he described his work. There was excitement in his eyes when he talked about the places he had visited and the sights he had seen. Sunsets in Alaska. Beggars in the streets of Mexico City. A gathering of elephants on an African plain.

After meeting his family, she had wondered how he could have left them. After listening to him talk about what he did, she knew that he had had to. The urge to wander was an intrinsic part of him, as much a trait as his dark hair or the cleft in his chin.

His mother understood that. On Friday night she invited Jonah and Maggie to dinner. They ate pot roast, served with a generous helping of proud stories about Jonah. He was obviously embarrassed and begged her to change the subject, but she was not to be deterred.

"He walked when he was ten months old," Carrie Pendleton told Maggie. "And went straight out the back door, which his father had left open. That's where Jonah has been headed ever since. Out." If there was a hint of sadness in her smile, there was also acceptance.

Yet Maggie was already beginning to dread the inevitable day when he would leave. She cursed herself for the feeling. She prayed for it to go away. It merely grew, in direct proportion to the minutes she spent with him.

And still he didn't make a move to touch her. In fact, he went out of his way not to. But he couldn't always control the way he looked at her. Maggie wondered what he would think if she told him that just a glance from his blue eyes left her damp and aching. She didn't know what to think of it herself. No one had ever affected her quite this way.

By the first week of November she was sure she was losing her mind. She dressed for a mid-morning appointment with a client and lectured herself. "Tonight I'm not going to be home when he comes knocking on my door. I'll call Liz. I'll let her walk me to death around the track and burn off some of those cookies I've been eating. Tomorrow I'll go visit Eugenia. He'll stop coming by. I'll forget him." Maggie leaned against the edge of her antique oak dresser, staring at her reflection in the mirror. "Please, God," she whispered. "Please let me forget I ever met Jonah Pendleton."

She knew that wouldn't happen. Just as she wasn't going to forget that moment they had shared at Eugenia's party. The way his fingers had felt against her skin. In her hair. The ache Jonah had started inside of her wasn't going to leave. Even when he did.

"Sex," she told her reflection. "No big deal. Just pure, undiluted sexual desire. You can handle that, Maggie. Sure you can." But her hands were shaking as she slipped on her favorite rust-colored sweater dress. She put on her pearls and fluffed out her hair and tried to think about something, anything but Jonah. "Thank heavens," she muttered when the phone rang. Maybe this would be something that would distract her completely.

But the caller was Jonah.

His voice was low but frantic. "Maggie, I hate to impose. I know you're busy, but I really need a favor."

"Okay."

"There's a set of blueprints up in my apartment, on the coffee table. Michael doesn't know I have them. I took them off his desk yesterday so I could study them. I'm afraid he's bidding too low on another big job."

"Oh, no."

Jonah sighed. "Yeah. Another disaster in the making. He was looking for them earlier but got called out to a job site. Is there any way you can get them over to me? He'll be back before I can get home to pick them up."

Maggie stifled the urge to tell him his spying on Michael was getting out of hand. There had to be some other way of trying to help his brother. "Sure," she agreed, glancing at her watch. She could probably postpone her meeting until later this afternoon. "I'll be there soon."

"Be careful, but please hurry, okay? I owe you one."

It was raining and traffic was snarled, and it took Maggie twice as long as she had expected to get to Pendleton Construction's headquarters. The building was an unpretentious, square brick structure with bulldozers and other equipment parked in a fenced lot at the rear. Clutching the blueprints under her raincoat, Maggie dashed across the parking lot. Jonah met her at the door.

Unfortunately, Michael came in right behind her.

Maggie thought Jonah's brother looked tired. Water dripped from his hair and down his orange poncho. There was mud on his boots, and his handsome features were set in grim lines as he checked through a stack of messages on the receptionist's desk. He spoke to a man, obviously another employee, who was also standing by the desk. Then he stared hard at Jonah.

"You remember Maggie, don't you, Michael?" Jonah did his best to make the blueprints appear inconspicuous.

Michael nodded in her direction. "Of course. Hello again." His gaze went directly to the prints, and he looked askance at Jonah.

"Just something I left at home," Jonah explained nonchalantly. "I asked Maggie to bring it in."

Michael's eyes blazed with ill-concealed fury, and his resemblance to Jonah became more pronounced. "Could those be the Anderson job prints?"

Now Jonah's lips thinned. He tossed the prints to his brother. "Sure. That's exactly what they are. And I'd like to talk to you about them."

Maggie saw the look that passed between the receptionist and the other man. Even more than the tension in the air, that look told her there was going to be trouble between the Pendleton brothers. She had two choices—she could leave or try to help. She chose the latter.

"Jonah," she said, physically stepping between the two men. "You promised to take me to lunch, remember?"

Michael, however, was having none of her interference. "Excuse me, Maggie, but before he takes you anywhere I need to have a word with my brother." He started down the hall. "Let's talk, Jonah."

"Jonah..." Maggie touched his arm, but he shook her off and followed his brother to an office at the end of the hall. The windows in the front office rattled as the door slammed behind him. And for a moment it was so quiet, Maggie could hear the receptionist breathe.

"Oh, dear."

Maggie turned. Carrie Pendleton was standing in the doorway to another office. She frowned for a moment, gazing down the hall. Then she smiled at Maggie. "Why don't you wait in my office for Jonah?"

Once they were in Carrie's office, well away from the receptionist, Maggie came clean. "We weren't really going to lunch. I was just hoping to prevent a confrontation."

"Getting between two charging bulls might be safer." Carrie took a seat behind her desk and put a hand to her graying hair. "I guess you know all about our troubles around here."

Maggie shifted her weight from one foot to the other. She really didn't know how much of what Jonah had told her she should reveal.

"It's okay," Carrie said, gesturing toward a chair in front of her desk. "I'm kind of glad Jonah has confided in you. He won't talk to me very much. And Michael won't talk to him." The sound of raised voices drifted down the hall. Her smile was wry. "He does yell on occasion, however."

"Jonah just wants to help."

"Of course he does. And he could, too, if Michael would let him." Carrie rubbed at her temples. "One of these days Jonah will get tired of trying, and he'll walk out. Go back to what he loves doing."

Because she knew that was exactly what would happen, Maggie said nothing. She didn't want to think about the day Jonah would leave. Instead she glanced around the office. Most of one wall was covered with a Plexiglas panel. Beneath it were snapshots. Dozens of them. She stood to look at them. They showed Jonah and Michael as youngsters in cowboy outfits, baseball uniforms, playing with a dog, blowing out candles on birthday cakes, with their arms around a younger Carrie and laughing with a tall, handsome man who had to be their father.

"Quite a collection, isn't it?" Carrie said, coming to stand beside her. "It's not likely I'll forget anything about my boys, with this collage to look at."

"As if you'd forget anything, anyway," Maggie murmured.

Nodding, Carrie tapped the glass that covered a picture of Jonah and Michael in front of a Christmas tree. "They were ten and eight here. See that red wagon Michael is in? Jonah pulled him around in that for months. Everywhere Jonah went, everything he did, that's where Michael wanted to be, what he wanted to do. Jonah was awfully patient with him." Her finger stroked over the faces in another close-up candid shot, this one of two teenaged boys and a girl. The girl and Jonah were clowning for the camera, their cheeks pressed close together.

Maggie looked closely at the picture, interested not in some girl from Jonah's past but in the look on Michael's face. She wondered if Carrie, with her mother's eye, could see the envy in Michael's face, the pure resentment in his narrowed eyes. Of course Maggie could be wrong. Photographs could be deceiving. But she couldn't help thinking that the emotion preserved by film on Michael's teenaged face was the same one that raged in him now.

She had enough tenderness inside of her to sympathize with Michael. Even in the earlier photographs, Jonah's personality shone through. He was the one holding the biggest trophy, pictured with the prettiest girl, sporting the longest hair, even riding the flashier bicycle. Michael was always the more handsome. But somehow in every picture they shared, Jonah was the focus of attention.

From down the hall came the sound of a door being slammed open against the wall. Maggie and Carrie started out of the office, stopping in the doorway as Jonah stalked by. Michael came after him, red-faced and swearing.

"You don't know everything, Jonah," he shouted. "You weren't here, remember? And you're not going to be here. So just stay out of my business. *My* business, do you understand? *Mine.*"

"Son," Carrie began, catching his arm. "Please, don't—"

But Michael wasn't to be stopped. "Do you understand me, Jonah?"

At the front door, Jonah wheeled around. His voice was low. "I understand you, Michael," he sneered. "Loud and clear. And if you want to drive this place straight to hell, that's fine with me. But you're not taking Mom's security with you. That's one mistake Dad would never have let you make."

Michael turned white with anger and took another step forward. "You don't know what you're talking about. You don't have any idea who Dad was, much less what he planned for this place or for Mom. You were never here to talk to him, remember?"

A stricken look crossed Jonah's face. Then he turned, disappearing out the door and into the cold November rain.

Six

The slow, steady rain continued all afternoon. Jonah thought it appropriate that he spent the day slogging through mud at the new mall where *Michael's* company was putting in a parking lot. Mud was what this company was mired in. A quicksand of financial disaster, to be more exact.

He accomplished little at the sodden, muddy site. A change the mall's developer had requested required only a minor alteration in plans. All too soon Jonah was finished. He couldn't, wouldn't go back to the office. Not while Michael's final comment still stung. His brother had taken aim at Jonah's weak spot and scored a bull's-eye.

Anger had caused Michael to say Jonah hadn't known their father. Jonah was certain Michael was wrong. Wasn't he? The hint of a doubt began to eat away at Jonah's confidence as he thought of all the years he had been away. Then he put a stop to his runaway thoughts. If there was any truth at all in what Michael had said to him this morning, it was that Jonah didn't really know their father's exact plans for the company. They had rarely discussed that. Jonah, however, wasn't sure Michael knew those plans, either. Jonah couldn't believe that their father would have taken the risks that Michael had.

Depressed over the entire situation, Jonah left the mall's construction site and headed for home. He didn't pause to wonder why the house where he had lived only a few weeks—Maggie's house—should feel like home to him.

As the perfect ending to the day, his car overheated by the time he made it through the traffic to the quiet street. Cursing, he parked in his customary place, got out and opened the hood to see what the problem was. Steam rose from the radiator, and cold rain ran down Jonah's neck as he bent over for a closer look. Whatever was wrong would require more than a cursory glance to discover. "Damned rental car," he muttered and slammed the hood. He was still cursing when he stepped inside the entry foyer.

He ended his tirade when he saw Maggie in the doorway to her apartment. For the first time since he had slammed out of the office, he remembered that she had been waiting for him.

Her brown eyes were dark with concern. "Are you okay, Jonah?"

"Sure," he muttered. "I'm fine, except for still being mad as hell. I'm great, if you disregard the fact that I'm wet and cold and this weather has every bone I ever broke aching like hell."

She held out her hand. "Come on in. I've got a fire burning and some fresh coffee."

Jonah wanted to resist. Every instinct he possessed urged him to back away from Maggie. Today he was too dispirited and too tired to resist her feminine allure as he'd been doing for the past few weeks. Purposefully he had put himself to a test, forcing himself to spend time with her yet not touch her. What the test would prove he wasn't sure. Except perhaps to demonstrate how a man could function in a state of near perpetual arousal.

"Jonah, please come in."

He gazed a moment more at Maggie's outstretched hand. "I'm wet and muddy," he offered as a feeble excuse.

But she wasn't to be deterred, and he soon found himself at her kitchen table, drinking coffee, enjoying the delicious aroma of something she had baked and the warmth of the crackling fire.

"Move over to one of the chairs by the fireplace," Maggie suggested. "You'll warm up faster."

"I'll get mud on your upholstery."

"A little dirt will clean up."

Thinking again of the mire of business problems facing his brother, Jonah shook his head. "Not always."

Maggie set a plate of sliced bread on the table. "It's pumpkin bread," she explained and slipped into the seat beside him. They sat quietly together until she said, "Michael was very angry."

Jonah's laugh was tight. "I don't think angry is descriptive enough, Maggie."

"I'm sorry. I tried to get there as soon as I could. The traffic—"

"Don't worry about it. I shouldn't have forgotten the prints this morning." He bit into a warm slice of bread, appreciating the spiced flavor even as he stared at the rivulets of rain on the window above Maggie's kitchen sink. "I probably shouldn't have taken the prints to start with," he admitted after a long moment of silence had passed.

Maggie sighed and refilled her own coffee mug. "It just seems to me that you would get further with Michael if you could convince him to sit down and have a long, reasonable discussion."

"He doesn't want to talk to me."

"Your mother should be there, too."

"Mom is too emotionally involved. She gets too upset."

Maggie raised an eyebrow. "She's more emotional than you and Michael? Can she get more upset than your argument got her today?"

She had a point, Jonah conceded. He rubbed a hand through his damp hair and took a deep breath. "I shouldn't have lost my temper with him."

"Have you and Michael always argued like this?"

He shook his head. "We were buddies as kids. Did everything together for a long, long time." He grinned, remembering some of those times. "We were practically inseparable until I discovered girls."

Crumbling a piece of bread onto a napkin, Maggie looked thoughtful. "I bet you were the one who decided what games you and Michael played, where you went, who you went with."

Jonah frowned. "Maybe I was. Hell, it's only natural. I'm the older one. What are you getting at, Maggie?"

"It's just that Michael resents you so much—"

"That's not exactly an earth-shattering conclusion."

"Of course not. It's obvious. But what I'm getting at is that maybe he has always resented you. Because you were older. The leader." Her dimple creased her cheek. "Because you discovered girls first."

"So what?" Jonah said, puzzled. "That's kid stuff, Maggie. We're dealing with the real world now. The business world. Michael has depleted all the company's resources by trying to expand too quickly. And to make it worse, Mom has contributed all of the savings she and Dad had accumulated. If the company goes under she loses that, plus the income the firm brings her now. Now I can take care of her financially, but it's not my nature to stand idly by when the problems could be solved by exercising a little sense. Michael has got to stop behaving like some resentful child and let someone else in on some of the decisions."

Maggie's eyes narrowed. "In other words he should let big-brother Jonah swoop in, save the day and depart in a blaze of glory, right?"

"I didn't say that—"

"But it's what you meant," she insisted.

Jonah began to get irritated again. First there had been Michael's refusal to listen to sense this morning. Now here was Maggie, trying to tell him the situation was all his fault. He pushed away from the table. "Listen, I don't need—"

"Sure, tell me it's none of my business," she interrupted, getting to her feet, an unexpected flash of temper in her eyes. "It isn't my concern, except that you involved me today."

"You could have left."

She made an impatient gesture with her hands. "Yeah, that's what I do. I walk out on friends when they're in trouble."

"Now you're being melodramatic."

"And you're not being fair to your brother," she shot back at him.

Now he was really angry. He stood and shoved the chair back under the table, a bit harder than necessary. "I think we had better drop the entire subject, Maggie. Because you don't know what you're talking about."

The tilt of her chin was challenging. "Oh, really? Tell me, Jonah, is this the way you talk to Michael. Do you listen to him, or do you shove things around and tell him he doesn't know what he's talking about?"

The picture her words painted of him was all the more unflattering because it held a grain of truth. But that made Jonah angrier still. "Listen," he said, taking pains to try and keep his fury from showing in his voice. "All I do is try to make Michael see where he's screwing up."

Maggie laughed. "Oh, so first you tell him he's a screwup, right?" Shaking her head, she picked up her coffee mug and carried it to the sink. "That's a great way to handle someone whose cooperation you want."

"I don't need to *handle* him," Jonah retorted. "For God's sake, he's my brother, not some foreman on a crew that I'm trying to work with."

She wheeled around, a look of triumph on her face. "And because he's your brother, he doesn't deserve all the niceties or the respect you would use with any other colleague. Is that what you're trying to say, Jonah?"

The anger seeped out of him, replaced by guilt. He pulled the chair out from under the table again and sat down heavily, wishing what Maggie had said didn't make so much sense. "I've made one royal mess, haven't I?"

"It sounds to me as if Michael has made the mess. You just haven't been helping much."

"I try to tell him—"

"Tell?" Maggie crossed her arms and leaned against the counter, a smile playing about her mouth. "Have you ever tried asking instead of telling? Listening rather than talking?"

"I have tried," Jonah protested, though the minute he said the words he wondered if they were really true. "At least I think I have." He passed a hand over his face. "I guess I've done more harm than good. Michael will probably never listen to me."

"So what are you going to do? Give up?"

He responded to the faint censure in her words. "Hey, you're the one who just finished telling me how rotten I've been to him. What do you suggest I do?"

"How about eating some humble pie?"

"What?"

"You told me the night we got stuck on that elevator that you don't really know too much about building some of the things Michael has in the works. Approach him with questions."

"Oh yeah," Jonah agreed sarcastically. "That's exactly what I should say. Then Michael will have another chance to tell me I don't know sh—"

Maggie's laughter cut him off. "Jonah, surely with all of your overworked charm, you can find enough finesse to get around that. If you actually tried to engage Michael in a conversation instead of a confrontation, you might get somewhere."

Jonah's shoulders slumped again. She was right, of course, and it irritated the hell out of him. He should have been smart enough to realize he was using the wrong approach with Michael. "How did you get so smart, anyway?" he asked, glaring at Maggie with what was now mock anger.

"All women are smart this way." She smiled as she poured more coffee into his mug. "But only a few of us dispense our wisdom so freely to men. You're lucky that I was in a generous mood today."

They shared a moment of laughter, and Jonah was struck by the rightness of the scene. A cold day. A warm kitchen. A woman to share his troubles with. Not just any woman, of course. Maggie.

The phone rang, and she crossed the room to answer it. As always he noticed the grace of her movements, the friendliness of her laughter, the precise way she asked questions of the person, obviously a client, who had called. She was so . . . serene, he decided, for want of a better word. Growing up as she had, how had she retained her sweet disposition? Who had taught her how to make people feel so comfortable, so at ease in her home? Eugenia was the obvious answer, but Jonah sensed that Maggie's soothing instincts were inborn.

He had instincts, too, the kind that made his body stir in response to her as she turned from the phone and gave him that radiant smile.

"I love dealing with satisfied customers, don't you?" she asked.

Jonah murmured a reply and shifted in his seat. The ache in his injured shoulder deepened. His fingers couldn't quite reach the place where the pain was the worst, and he grunted in frustration.

Maggie frowned. "What's wrong?"

"The rain's got this shoulder acting up. No big deal."

"Nonsense." He protested but she was behind him quickly, her nimble fingers finding the place where he hurt. "Is that better?"

Jonah wasn't sure. The ache in her shoulder had abated somewhat, but other regions of his anatomy weren't being so cooperative. "Maggie, really," he said. "I just need to take a couple of aspirin—"

She snapped her fingers and was across the room quickly, giving him a tempting view of her rounded derriere as she rummaged in a low cabinet. "I've got some of that cream here, you know, the kind with aspirin in it. I used it the last time Liz talked me into attempting a real exercise program." She pulled a tube from the cabinet. "I knew it was here." She turned back to him. "I'll rub this in."

Aghast, he stood. He couldn't sit still while Maggie rubbed anything into his bare skin. "I have some of that, Maggie. I can do it—"

"Please don't be silly," she protested. "Take off your shirt."

Maybe it was the unintentional eroticism of hearing Maggie tell him to take off his clothes. Or maybe it was that the temptation to have her hands on his skin was too much for Jonah to bear. Whatever the reason, he stripped off his flannel shirt and sat down. Scrupulously he avoided meeting her eyes, but every muscle in his body stiffened, anticipating her touch.

What am I doing? Maggie asked herself as she squeezed a dollop of cream into her palm. Some self-destructive demon inside of her was setting her up for disaster. How could she stand here so blithely, watching the object of a dozen different sexual fantasies strip to the waist? Beyond that, how could she touch him?

Taking a deep breath, she focused only on the point just below his left shoulder... his broad, hard-muscled shoulder... covered by smooth, sleek skin. That he was in good shape didn't surprise her. He was on a program of rigorous exercises to build up the strength he had lost when his injuries had put him in the hospital. Sometimes at night, she heard a steady *thump, thump* from his apartment above hers, and she knew he was working out. She had tried not to think of him—nearly naked—with sweat glistening on his body. She had . . .

With a guilty start, she realized she had yet to apply the first bit of cream to his shoulder. He would think she was crazy, just standing here like a zombie. Yet the minute her hand touched him, Maggie knew without a doubt that the crazy part was not in hesitating but in touching him at all.

His skin was warm. And sleek. Easy to touch. As she rubbed the cream in, her other hand went automatically to his other shoulder, her fingers sliding across his back, pressing hard. Then lightly. Adopting a rhythm she hoped would soothe him. Please him. Her own pleasure came from just touching him.

Pleasure was the wrong word for what he was feeling, Jonah decided. It was also more than arousal. The sensations had a keener edge to them. Maybe it was the way a starving man feels when he finally gets a taste of food. It hurt too much to be enjoyed.

His eyes closed, and he drifted somewhere between fantasy and reality, savoring Maggie's light but strong touch. The fantasy was that they might go on like this forever. The reality was the knowledge that he would explode long before forever could even begin. Maggie's fingernails raked gently across his skin and he felt himself grow harder, heard his breathing grow ragged.

"Maggie...sweetheart," he muttered, turning around in the chair, managing to elude her touch for a moment. "If you don't stop..."

Her startled gaze met his. With her pink, trembling lips and flushed cheeks, she looked as if she needed to be kissed. More important, she looked as if she wanted to be kissed. This time, Jonah didn't ignore the invitation.

He stood, disregarding the way the sudden movement jarred his leg. The chair was in his way, so he shoved it aside. It screeched across the wooden floor as he pulled her close. Their gazes still locked, he surprised Maggie by tracing a finger along her jawline. The gesture was brief, unexpectedly tender. Then his hand was in her hair. And his mouth was on hers.

And I thought it was good the first time, she thought. That first kiss didn't compare with this. Nothing she had ever experienced could be likened to the ravenous need that ate through her body as Jonah's lips took hers. At the first touch of his mouth, there was a dampness between her legs. Maybe it was there before he touched her. The only thing she could be certain of was the way the pressure built inside her.

The touch of his fingers fueled that feeling. His hands were everywhere. On her face. Moving down her sides. Cupping her bottom while he ground his hips into hers.

"Dear God," Jonah murmured against her mouth. "Do you feel what you do to me, Maggie?"

Her answer was a tiny cry, uttered deep in her throat. Then her lips were on his again, her body was pushing against his, seeking an impossible intimacy.

Giving into frustration, Jonah dragged her dress upward till it bunched at her waist. Then he groaned at the impediment her panty hose presented. "Why do you women wear these damn things, anyway?" He caught Maggie's shocked gasp against his lips as he pushed one hand under the stretchy waistband. Beneath a final barrier of silk and lace, he found his goal—the smooth, naked skin of her curvy, tempting rear end.

Maggie felt as if all the air was being crushed from her lungs. She broke away from Jonah's kiss and buried her face in the light dusting of dark hair on his chest. Her lips grazed his skin, tasting the salt of perspiration. The smell of rain and hard work and sheer virility filled her head, adding to her arousal. Jonah's leg snaked between hers and she pressed downward, mindless of what she was doing, knowing only that every sensation in her body had focused in that one spot.

She lifted her mouth to his once more, and Jonah's hand closed around her breast. Her nipples were already so hard that his touch was almost painful, even through the layers presented by her dress and bra.

"I want to kiss you here," Jonah whispered. His thumb stroked the pebbled flesh again. "I'm going to kiss you here."

"Please," she said, drawing back to stare into his passion-darkened eyes. "Please, Jonah. Do."

Jonah never understood what made him pause. Every nerve of his body screamed for him to follow Maggie's urgent plea. To get them both out of their clothes. To back her up against the table edge. Take her breast in his mouth. And push himself deep inside of her. He was hard as a rock. Throbbing. More than ready.

So why did he stop? It had something to do with Maggie's trusting brown eyes and the open, unself-conscious way in which she was about to share herself with him. One time with this woman wouldn't be enough, he told himself. Not once, not a hundred. But sometime it would have to be enough, because someday he would walk away from here. And when he did, the trust in her eyes would turn to hurt. That wasn't a sight Jonah wanted to carry with him.

So he pulled away from her. He turned around, grabbed his jacket and walked out the door, telling himself he was doing it for her, yet knowing it was his own sense of self-preservation that really moved him.

Maggie stood where Jonah had left her for a long time. She didn't know why she hadn't said something to him, called him back, called him names. She wanted to. She wanted to slap him, laugh at him as if this had all been a joke. She wanted to tell him she hadn't really wanted him, anyway.

He had wanted her, that much she knew for sure. Then she had done something wrong. But what? Color warmed her cheeks as she remembered her response to him. Had she responded too well? Not enough? She just didn't know.

As soon as she gathered her scattered senses, Maggie went about her business. She smoothed her clothes, tidied the kitchen and stoked the fire. She spent several hours going over notes she had taken about an office suite she was designing. She turned through several fabric sample books and read a brochure about an upcoming antique auction.

Only when she ran out of things to do did Maggie curl up in her chair in front of the fireplace and stare at the ceiling. There was enough spite in her to hope that Jonah's ache was as hard and as insistent as hers.

The sun's afternoon rays had turned the tree outside Jonah's office into a halo of orange. Most other trees had surrendered their leaves to November's chilly wind. This one hung on, however, evidently not caring that the earth was moving into another season.

"As if trees *care* about anything," Jonah muttered. Something had gotten into him this week. He had taken to staring out this window for long stretches of time. Perhaps that was why he felt as if the tree were a personal friend whose thoughts he could read. Maggie would say...

He caught himself before the thought was completed. Maggie would say nothing to him after what had happened last week. Not that he had given her any opportunity. He had snuck out early in the morning, come home late at night. He didn't want to explain himself to her. Most importantly, he didn't want to be tempted into playing out that scene again.

The memory of Maggie in his arms, of her satin skin beneath his hands still had the capacity to excite him. God, how she had made him burn. Even after walking away from her he had been excited. To alleviate the ache he had used the only means a man had available: straight shots of liquor and pointless flirtations with women at bars. Such substitutes, never really satisfactory, had been poor indeed when compared to Maggie.

He moved from the window and turned his attention to the computer beside his desk, trying to concentrate on the figures Michael had given him earlier that day. Jonah had decided to give Maggie's ideas about his brother a try. There had been no instant capitulation, but they had stopped shouting at each other every time they tried to discuss a problem. The result was that Michael had finally asked for Jonah's opinion. It was a small start, but at least it was a start.

"You look busy," his mother said from the doorway.

Jonah looked up at her and smiled. "I'm not really. I think all this sunshine is distracting me."

"Maybe." There was ripe speculation in his mom's gaze as she stepped into the room. "I haven't heard you mention Maggie this week. What'd we do, scare her off when you and Michael had your last round?"

"Maggie doesn't scare that easily."

"That's what I thought, but you haven't mentioned her."

He looked back at the computer. "I haven't seen her."

"Oh." The small word carried the full force of his mother's disapproval.

"Mom, please don't start."

She ignored him, of course. "You could do worse than Maggie O'Grady."

"I agree."

"Then what's wrong with you?" Carrie put her hands on her hips, frowning at him. "You leave a woman like that alone for a week and she might just be snatched up by someone else."

Jonah forced himself to shrug. "Those are the risks, I guess."

Carrie sniffed. "All right, son, as long as you know what you might be throwing away."

He knew what he had thrown away, all right. A treasure, as Eugenia might put it. He told himself it was for the best, but that was small compensation for his loneliness. Dammit, he missed Maggie. As far as he had traveled, as long as he had sometimes stayed away from those people most important to him, he couldn't remember missing anyone this badly.

Breaking the habit he had set during the last week, Jonah went straight home that afternoon. He had been spending too much time in bars, drinking too much tequila. Careful men who were concerned about living no longer searched for casual contact in such places. Jonah, however, had been dismayed to realize he didn't even enjoy looking. Every blonde he saw reminded him of Maggie.

So tonight he went home, hoping not to see her, wondering exactly what he would do with himself all evening. In the foyer outside Maggie's door he paused for a moment, stopped by the angry voices coming from inside. He frowned, trying to hear what was being said. He recognized Maggie's voice, though he had never heard it raised to quite this level before. She was arguing with another woman. Telling himself it was none of his business, he placed one foot on the first step. Then Maggie's door burst open.

The woman who stalked out was tall, flamboyantly dressed in a purple cape and obviously furious. She stopped at the front door to say, "You, my dear, don't understand the concept of style."

From her doorway, Maggie retorted, "Unfortunately I know plenty about real style. That's why I don't want to work with you."

"Fine." With a twirl of her cape the woman made her departure, leaving the front door standing wide open.

"Some people," Maggie muttered. She crossed the hall and closed the door. When she looked up, she saw Jonah.

He gulped, tried to greet her, but ended up just standing there. Maggie, however, was in perfect control of herself.

"Wait right here," she told him and disappeared into her apartment. She came back, holding the flannel shirt he had left in her kitchen. It had been washed and ironed and was now folded into a perfect square.

"Thanks," he said feebly as he took it from her.

"No problem." Maggie's gaze was cool as she held his. "You doing okay?"

"Yes."

"No problems in the apartment?"

"None." He swallowed. God, this was so awful. He couldn't stand here, talking to her as if she were a stranger. "Maggie," he began.

"We'll see you around, okay?" she said brightly. Then her door clicked shut.

Jonah wanted to punch the wall. He settled for reducing the shirt he held to a crumpled mess.

Maggie slumped against her door, listening to his footsteps disappear upstairs. She hated this. *Hated it*. She had handled this encounter just fine, but what happened next time? She wished he would move. Just knowing he was in the house, living right above her head, crowded her. She was aware of his every coming and going. If she had been bothered by him before last week, now she was hypersensitive. The tension she felt had her doing crazy things.

"Like throwing paying customers out the door," she whispered and groaned in frustration.

It didn't matter that Mrs. Sharnelle had wanted to do her home completely in mixed shades of purple and orange. Maggie had handled tougher requests than that. It wasn't important that the woman hadn't liked any of the fabrics Maggie had selected. That was the nature of the business. Maggie had no excuse for behaving so badly to her. Maybe she could call tomorrow and apologize.

"Oh, what the hell," she said to the empty room. She didn't want to deal with Mrs. Sharnelle or anyone else. She was dissatisfied with her work, her home, her entire life.

And all because of Jonah Pendleton.

Maggie headed for her kitchen, wondering how she had allowed her entire existence to be turned on its end by a man who was nothing like the man she had always dreamed of. He was a rambler. And a gypsy.

And she was crazy about him.

Don had been right, Maggie realized. Don was the man she had dated for the better part of six months, but when he proposed, she had refused. He had told her she was fooling herself, that she was at heart too restless for the security or comfort she claimed to desire. In their last, bitter scene, he had urged her to "...have an affair. Something raw and basic and physical. Get that out of your system, and then call me."

Maggie wasn't sure just when or why Don had arrived at his conclusions about her true nature. But it looked as if he had been correct. For she wanted something raw and basic and physical. She wanted Jonah. Just the taste she'd had of him had spoiled her for safe, predictable types such as Don. Even though Jonah didn't want her, she was never going to be the same.

From the floor above came a rhythmic *thump, thump*. Jonah was exercising, she thought. It took no imagination at all to see or feel the play of his muscles beneath his skin.

Snatching up her purse, Maggie escaped from the house and her treacherous thoughts.

Her aimless wandering took her to the mall, where she had her hair cut at one of those no-appointment salons. The cut she received was no big change. But since the same person had been styling her hair for as long as she could remember, Maggie felt downright subversive.

She flashed her credit cards in shops up and down the mall corridor, not leaving until she was shooed out by an exhausted store manager. The bags Maggie carried bulged with trendy clothes, exactly the opposite of the classic styles she favored.

She didn't admit to feeling any better, however, until she stopped at a fast-food place for a hamburger, fries and a double-chocolate shake.

The next day she went to Eugenia's for afternoon tea. She wore a black leather skirt teamed with a fringed suede jacket and black boots. Maggie had never worn anything like this in her life. She arrived late, hoping to make an entrance, wondering just what her friends would have to say about her.

Expectantly she paused in the doorway of the small front parlor. Liz, Cassandra and Eugenia looked up at her. But no one said a word about her outfit.

"Maggie, thank God you're finally here," Cassandra said, bouncing up from her seat on the sofa. "I was going to burst if you had been a minute later."

Disappointed that the spotlight had been stolen from her, Maggie walked in and dropped into a chair. She viewed her sister-in-law with resignation. "What'd you do this time, Cassandra?"

"It's great news." With the drama only she could muster, Cassandra whirled to the center of the room. "I . . . I mean, we . . . Daniel and I . . ."

"For God's sake, what?" Maggie snapped.

Eugenia and Liz looked at her in consternation.

Cassandra, however, didn't appear to know Maggie had spoken. She was too intent on her announcement. And her words broke over Maggie like a bomb. She had to ask Cassandra to repeat them.

"It's true," Cassandra trilled giddily. "We're having a baby!"

Seven

She should have been happy. Her brother was going to be a father; one of her dearest friends, a mother. Maggie wanted to be ecstatic. But only one thought kept running through her head.

This should be me.

She didn't mean that Cassandra wasn't going to be a wonderful mother. Cassandra was sunshine and rainbows and everything exciting. She would fill her child's life with magic and love. And Daniel. Oh, but he would be the best father. Cassandra, his only love, had made him laugh again. Now they were having a family. That would make up for all the hurt Daniel had known.

And as for Maggie's hurt... Well, she told herself, that had nothing to do with this happy moment.

Liz was hugging Cassandra. Eugenia went out in the hall, calling for Jeannette, ordering champagne. And still Maggie sat in her chair, trying to remove the lead balloon that seemed to have landed on her chest.

"I can't believe it." Liz clapped her hands. "Now you're sure, aren't you, Cassandra? You aren't jumping to conclusions?"

Cassandra nodded. "I'm two months pregnant. The doctor confirmed it today. I've been dying to tell all of you, but I wanted to be a hundred percent positive before I got anyone's hopes up."

"You didn't waste any time, I'll say that much of you."

Patting her flat stomach, Cassandra grinned. "We're calling it our honeymoon baby."

"What about Daniel?" Liz pressed. "Is he just going through the roof or what?"

"He's on his way over here now. You can see for yourself." Cassandra hugged Liz again. "I never thought I'd be the first one . . ." She stopped abruptly, a guilty flush creeping up her neck as she stared at Maggie. "Maggie, I'm sorry. I didn't mean . . ."

Maggie knew then that she had to get up from her chair and say something. Cassandra's happiness and excitement shouldn't be clouded by any reminder of sorrow. "It's okay," she said softly, rising. She went to Cassandra and put her arms around her. She put all the love she felt for this happy-go-lucky sprite into her hug. "I'm thrilled for you. Really, really thrilled."

Cassandra's dark eyes, however, were clouded as she drew away. "But Maggie, I didn't mean . . . I . . . none of us . . . we haven't forgotten Rachel."

"Of course we haven't," Liz added.

Tears stung Maggie's eyes as she squeezed Liz's hand with her own. The conflicting emotions of joy and sadness filled her to overflowing. She didn't trust herself to speak, so she just held on to her two best friends.

Eugenia returned before the moment could get any more emotional. "Goodness, what are these tears about?" she demanded. "This is a celebration."

Jeannette bustled in the door behind Eugenia, her plump face beaming. She carried a tray with a bottle of champagne and Eugenia's prized Waterford crystal goblets. "A *bébé*," she said. "A blessing from God."

"Most certainly," Eugenia agreed. Then she began firing instructions like a field marshal. "Pop the cork, Jeannette. Liz, you pour. None for you, Cassandra. You have to think of the baby. Jeannette can bring you some milk. And Maggie smile, you're going to be an aunt."

Smile, smile, smile. Maggie kept repeating that instruction over and over. And she obeyed it. Daniel arrived before the first toast was proposed, and she hugged him hard. "Congratulations."

He touched her face, gentleness in his expression. "You think I'm ready for this father thing?"

"Absolutely."

He pressed a kiss on her forehead, an astounding gesture for the normally undemonstrative Daniel. For too many years he had locked his feelings away, held himself apart from everyone who cared for him. Tears again flooded Maggie's eyes, not just because she loved her brother but because even that love couldn't completely erase the jealousy she was feeling.

This wasn't like her. She wasn't a jealous person. She had done what she could with the curves life had fired in her direction. But right now she felt like a rookie batter stepping up to the plate in the ninth inning with the bases loaded and everything riding on whether her bat could connect with a small white ball. No time for mistakes, a tiny voice seemed to whisper.

Dismissing her fatalistic thoughts, Maggie raised her glass as Eugenia made the toast to a new generation. The champagne went down easily, but even a second glass didn't improve Maggie's attitude. She tried hard, however, throwing herself into the spirit of the gathering, attempting to lose herself in the conversation and laughter. Liz's husband, Nathan, appeared before tea was over, and everyone ended up staying at Eugenia's for a celebratory dinner. It was a night like a hundred others she had known, but for one of the few times in her life, Maggie felt separated from the people she had loved so long and so well.

Unreasonably the one person she wanted to be with was Jonah.

But he didn't want her.

When she could stand the gaiety no longer, she made her excuses. Liz was the one who followed her to the door.

"Are you okay, Maggie?"

Maggie summoned a smile, the last one required of her for the night, she hoped. "I'm fine." With a last goodbye she turned to open the door, but Liz stopped her again.

"I like your hair," she said, grinning. "But the leather-and-suede outfit, well . . ."

"Go back to the party," Maggie told her, laughing a little as she went out into the cool November night.

In her car, she brushed a hand across her black leather skirt. It had been a silly purchase. She was being a silly, emotional woman. She was only thirty-one. She had no reason to feel as if her life was over or that she would never again know the happy expectation Cassandra was experiencing right now.

But no matter how she lectured herself. Maggie was crying by the time she opened the front door to her apartment. She cursed those tears, and she cursed the foolishness that allowed her to pull a framed photo from a drawer in her bedside table.

The sight of that small, incredibly *wanted* face brought her a fresh rush of pain. It just wasn't fair.

Clutching the photo, she lay on the bed and sobbed. Cried until she had no tears left, until she fell asleep.

Jonah was falling. He felt his feet sliding along the steel girder. He caught a dizzying glimpse of the ground, so far away. Then there was that horrifying feeling of nothingness....

He woke with a start and rolled over, his gaze going to the luminous hands of his alarm clock. Not long after midnight. He hadn't been asleep that long, but that wasn't surprising. When he dreamed of the fall, it was always early. It was as if his subconscious tried to get all the bad things out of the way up front. Then, if he was lucky, he could turn over and go right to sleep.

Tonight he had no such luck. He hadn't been tired when he went to bed in the first place. Having gone to sleep at all was a surprise. Now he was more awake than ever. What he wanted badly was a shot of tequila and a smoke.

The first requirement was easily found. The second, however, would necessitate a trip to his car, where he had left his cigars. He had hoped by leaving them there to start breaking the habit again. The yearning of a smoke overrode the warm comfort of his apartment, and Jonah pulled on jeans, a sweatshirt and shoes. Nothing, not a television or a voice, breached the silence of the house as he slipped downstairs. His neighbors, including Maggie, all appeared to be asleep. He was in the front foyer when he noticed Maggie's apartment door standing open.

He paused, frowning, listening to see if he could hear anything unusual. Again, the only sounds were the normal creaks and groans of this big, old house. Maybe she had just forgotten to lock up, he decided. Maggie was so trusting, and the other tenants, a couple of graduate students and an aspiring country-music singer, were people she had known for a long time. But still he had never seen that door open before. Without another moment's pause, he stepped into her darkened, little-used living room. "Maggie?" he said softly, moving farther inside.

There was no answer.

She's not even here, he told himself. However, in the light from the foyer he noticed her purse lying on the table by the door. Her keys glinted in the light, too. *So she's asleep, and she left the door open by mistake.* He turned to leave, trying to be as silent as possible. Then he stumbled on something, and to keep from falling he had to grab the back of a chair.

"What the hell?" He picked up a high-heeled, black suede boot. Strange. Neat-as-a-pin Maggie would never leave shoes lying at the door, as if she had pulled them off and carelessly dropped them. He had seen her himself, straightening up, setting to rights a room that was already in perfect order. Something here wasn't right.

"Maggie," he called, louder this time. There was no response. Unease quickened his pulse.

On the off chance that his imagination was just working overtime, Jonah crept through the apartment quietly. He felt like a sneak. Maggie might very well be asleep in her bedroom. But he had to make sure. The strength of his protective urge was overpowering, but he didn't pause to analyze the feeling.

In her ruffled, floral-scented room the light was on, but her bed, however rumpled, was empty. So was the kitchen. A cold November breeze blew in from the open back door. The lamp shining through her bedroom partially illuminated the porch. That, with the aid of a harvest moon, shed enough light for Jonah to make out Maggie's blanket-shrouded figure, sitting motionless in one of her rockers.

Something *was* wrong. He could see it in the tilt of her head. He could sense it.

Jonah paused in the doorway for a long moment, unsure of what to do. If she was upset, the last person she would want to see was him. She had made it clear with her bright and impersonal act yesterday that she wasn't going to let him close again.

Yet he couldn't leave her out there like this.

Pulling the door shut behind him, he stepped onto the porch.

Her head swiveled slowly in his direction, as if she wasn't really surprised to see him.

"Maggie?" Jonah said, stepping closer. "What are you doing out here?"

Her voice was flat, emotionless. "It's my porch."

He shifted from foot to foot, uncomfortably aware of the cold. "I found your front door open. I thought something had happened. I called—"

"I heard you."

"So why didn't you answer?"

Her shoulders moved under the quilt and she turned her attention back to the yard. He got the feeling he had been dismissed.

"What's wrong, Maggie?"

She said nothing, and he stepped closer. Had someone died? Was she ill? "Maggie, there's obviously something very wrong. I wish you would tell me."

"Go away, Jonah."

"But—"

"Please, go."

Faint irritation nudged his concern aside. "Come on, Maggie, you know I'm not leaving. To paraphrase something you once told me, I don't walk out on friends when they're in trouble."

She looked at him again. "We're not friends."

"Yes, we are." Not even bothering to ask her permission, he dragged a chair close to hers and sat. "What happened between us the other day doesn't mean I haven't come to care about you."

Her silence was colder than the wind.

Before he dragged whatever was wrong out of her, Jonah knew he was going to have to explain why he had walked out on her last week. "About what happened," he began.

"I don't want to talk about that."

"But I have to explain. It just wasn't right. We can't get involved."

"I understand."

He glanced at her sharply. "Do you?"

Her laugh was brittle. "Everyone is entitled to change his mind, Jonah."

"Yes, but the important thing is the reason I changed my mind."

"I'm well aware of why. I know I'm probably not your usual type. You remembered that in the nick of time. I should thank you."

"That's not exactly how I would explain it—"

"And I don't really care about what happened or why you left."

"Don't you?" The harsh words burst out before he could consider them. "You certainly didn't behave like someone who didn't care. You kissed like you wanted it, wanted it bad."

Her chair rocked forward and she jumped up, her quilt pooling on the porch. He was on his feet just as quickly, however, and he caught her before she could go inside.

"I'm sorry," he muttered, swinging her around to face him. "Maggie, I shouldn't have said that. I'm sorry. It wasn't like that, and I know it." In the moonlight, tears glinted on her downcast eyelashes. He felt like the worst kind of heel. His hands slid up to her shoulders. "Please, Maggie, look at me. I'm sorry."

Her eyes were full of misery, and now that he was this close to her, he could see that she had been crying. She tried to shrug away. "Let me go, Jonah."

"But I've hurt you, and that was exactly what I never wanted to do."

"Please, Jonah, just..." Her voice caught on a sob, and he drew her to him.

Maggie let her body go limp, forgetting for the moment the harsh words they had exchanged. All evening she had been yearning for Jonah's touch. For his comfort. She was going to give herself this much. She had had her night of self-pity. Now she could self-destruct, too. There was nothing more masochistic than allowing herself to be held by the man she wanted but who didn't want her. She would give in to the urge. Just for now. Just for tonight.

His fingers beneath her chin lifted her face. His voice was roughened velvet. "What is it? What are you doing out here all alone in the cold?"

"Cassandra's having a baby," Maggie said, as if that explained everything.

The puzzled line between Jonah's eyebrows didn't disappear. "And?"

Again she pressed her face to his strong, broad chest. God, now her jealousies seemed sillier and pettier than ever.

"What has that got to do with you?" Jonah prodded.

It was hard to lie when she looked into his blue eyes, so Maggie told the truth. "I wish it were me."

He continued to stare at her and Maggie pushed away from him, feeling like four kinds of a fool. "I'm sorry," she said. "It's not something I would expect you to understand. I'm just feeling old—"

"Maggie," he remonstrated softly. "That's nonsense."

"I know, but it feels..." She pressed a hand to her chest. "It feels like somebody stole my dreams, you know."

"No, I don't know." He spread his hands wide. "Maggie, if I had to put any money on the matter, I'd pick you as the woman most likely to become a mother. The right man will come along and—"

"I was a mother."

He blinked at her. "What?"

"I had a daughter." The pain in Maggie's chest intensifed. She took a deep breath, but the pain didn't change. "Her name was Rachel. She was three months old when she died."

Death, divorce, disappointment. The real world. Clearly, Jonah remembered the day Maggie had told him she knew about such things. It was after he had taunted her about living in a safe little vacuum. He was even more ashamed of that now.

"Please don't get me wrong," she told him. "I'm not a mental case. I haven't been mourning my child for ten years. Days, weeks go by when I don't even think of her. But tonight..." She bit her lip. "Tonight, I felt cheated."

Down the street a door slammed and a dog barked. The wind brought the scent of wood smoke and rattled the drying leaves that were left on the trees in the backyard. Totally immune to the cold, Jonah watched Maggie turn and lean against the porch's wooden railing.

"I had the simple dream," she whispered. "Liz wanted to save the world. Cassandra wanted to entertain it. I just wanted a family. And tonight I let myself get angry because my dreams haven't come true. I'm ashamed of that."

"How?" Jonah asked, still focused on the child she had lost. "How did Rachel die?"

Maggie turned and shook her head. "One minute she was breathing. Sleeping. The next..." Her voice broke. "I went in to feed her, and she was still. Completely still. So...still." She shuddered.

The horror was fresh in her voice. The sound went straight to Jonah's soul. A child had died. It was the sort of tragedy you read about and heard about all the time. You sighed over it, said it was a shame, and then you forgot it. Until you looked into the face of someone who had lived with the sorrow. That put a whole new slant on it. Especially when you considered how a child of Maggie O'Grady's would have been wanted, loved, treasured. For her, it must have felt as if someone had ripped out her heart.

How had she coped? My God, where did this woman get her strength? Jonah wondered. She had grown up in the midst of a storm. Her dreams had been snatched away. Yet she was ashamed of feeling angry and jealous, emotions that most people relied upon regularly.

He didn't attempt to offer words of comfort for a grief he couldn't imagine. Instead he picked up the blanket she had dropped. He slipped it carefully around her shoulders. Maggie's arms gathered his body close. She was cold. So was he. The blanket offered scant warmth. Yet the heat started the moment he touched her.

His mouth found hers easily. He didn't think about kissing her. He just did it. Without fuss or preamble or intent. Lips opened. Tongues danced in a rhythm so perfect it could only have been natural. For nothing is ever intentionally this right, Jonah thought. You couldn't plan perfection.

He loosened his grip on the blanket and it fell away, unnoticed, as his hands framed her face. He held her still, deepening the kiss, asking questions he didn't want to ask, receiving answers he didn't want to understand. With his hands in her hair, he drew away. He had to maintain his sanity this time.

But Maggie would have none of that. This was her night to indulge. The chance might not come again. "No, Jonah. Don't do that." Her arms tightened around his waist. Her hands gripped the material of his sweatshirt. "Please, don't be gallant this time. I don't want you to be smart. Be foolish." Leaning up, she put her lips to the vertical dent in his chin. She had wanted to do that for forever.

"Oh God, Maggie." He lifted her mouth to his again and lost most of his resolve in the process. "We shouldn't," he muttered, in between the kisses he pressed on her throat. Sweet heaven, the way she smelled. Like a piece of spring in the dead of winter.

"I'm sick of shouldn'ts." Maggie pushed her hands under his shirt, eager for the feel of his skin. "I want that," she whispered as his hand slipped over her breast. Her fingers slid down and cupped his firm behind. She pulled him forward, sighing, "And this, too." She laughed softly. "I want it *bad*, Jonah. The way I wanted it last week."

She heard his deep chuckle against her throat. Then he tugged her sweater free of her skirt. His fingers were cold against the skin of her midriff. She pulled back slightly as he fumbled with the center clasp of her bra. "Dammit, Maggie, my fingers are frozen stiff."

"Let me." Without ceremony she unhooked her bra and closed his hand around one full, warm breast.

Jonah didn't know if anything had ever felt as sweet. But the feeling was no sweeter than the sound of Maggie's soft moan of pleasure. His thumb brushed across her tightened nipple and her breath hissed out, a frozen cloud against the darkness.

"We're going to die of exposure," he murmured.

"Then come inside."

The simple invitation was a lighted fuse. It slipped through him, setting off explosive possibilities. Yes, he wanted inside. Inside Maggie. Taking her hand, he led her into the kitchen, to her bedroom.

After having sat on the porch for over an hour, Maggie was so cold the warmth of the indoors stung her face and her feet like match strikes. But that was nothing next to the anticipation that pushed along her nerves. Had she ever wanted anyone the way she wanted Jonah? Her marriage seemed distant, the passion she must have felt clouded by time and disappointment. Her few other experiences were simply inconsequential when compared to the want that gripped her now.

She was so overwhelmed it never occurred to her to switch off the lamp that burned on her bedside table. She didn't think about being shy or hesitant. Not that Jonah gave her a chance for that. He seemed to know instinctively that boldness was what pleased Maggie most.

Though he had rushed her through the apartment, his movements were slow as they stood beside her bed. His kiss was deep, lingering. With careful hands he drew her sweater over her head and pushed her bra straps down her arms. He tossed the lace and satin aside and allowed his gaze to caress her breasts. His hands followed, starting at her waist, slipping ever so slowly upward. He touched her the way a connoisseur might worship a coveted sculpture. With awe. And wonder.

His eyes, however, were steady on hers as his fingertips skimmed the valley between her breasts. "The fantasies weren't even close."

"Fantasies?"

"About you. About this." He cupped one breast and bent, capturing the aching peak in his mouth. He washed the nipple with his tongue until she trembled. Then greedily he repeated the loving strokes on her other breast.

Maggie knew she would have fallen if his arms hadn't been around her. Her arousal was that sharp. That demanding. The need sapped the strength from her bones, reusing it in the tidal wave of warmth that radiated from the juncture of her thighs. Didn't he feel the same throbbing demand?

Her hands pushed at the jeans that rode low on his narrow hips. The snap was already undone, as if he had dressed in haste. Beneath his jeans he wore nothing except the proof of how much he wanted her. She eased his pants down his hips, and his breath caught, his mouth moving from her breast to her shoulder. His teeth nipped her skin lightly as she took his sex in her hand.

Her sigh of satisfaction made Jonah chuckle. "Pleased?" he whispered.

"For the moment." She looked down, her fingers stroking his hot velvet length.

"And the moment will be over if you keep that up."

"Keep what up?" she teased.

He laughed, taking her mouth again as he pushed her hands away.

He tastes like liquor and sin, Maggie thought. *Just like the first night when he kissed me for Eugenia's benefit.* His tongue plumbed deep, his fingers caressed her breast, and to herself she said, *Thank you, Eugenia.*

They drew apart. But their gazes remained locked as haste replaced caution. Jonah tossed his sweatshirt in the corner. With shaking hands, Maggie stripped off her skirt. His jeans followed. Then her panties.

Jonah's gaze moved over her, pausing to appreciate the full breasts, the narrow waist, the womanly flare of her hips and thighs. Her hand slipped into his, trustingly. Had anyone ever trusted him so completely?

There was no time for an answer, however. Because the moment was lost to the sensations that came hard and fast as they fell to the bed. There was the cool slide of the cotton pillowcases beneath his back. The trickle of perspiration between Maggie's breasts. Its salty taste as he licked it away. Her moan of pleasure when he thrust upward into her.

She fit him like a glove. And rocked him to some place between this planet and the next.

But that was just the beginning.

He took her into a storm of loving. Maggie couldn't tell when the first downpour ended and the next began. One minute Jonah was filling her, emptying into her. A moment later—or was it a lifetime?—his hands were on her again. She couldn't quite believe that he was here with her. She didn't know how he had managed to tap into her most erotic thoughts. But with fingers and lips and tongue he built her passion higher. Till she begged him to stop.

He laughed, a wicked sound that only seemed to arouse her more. His mouth opened over her breast. His tongue stroked with something less than tenderness. "You want me to stop this, Maggie?"

Unable to speak, she shook her head.

Buried deep in the triangle of golden curls between her legs, his thumb stroked in a slow circle. "What about this, Maggie? Is this what you want stopped?"

She gasped her "No."

His thumb moved again. "What do you want, Maggie?" His other hand turned her face toward his. "Look at me. Tell me."

His eyes were so blue they were almost black. He looked as wild, as unconquered as the heroes in Jeannette's novels.

"Tell me, Maggie. What do you want?"

"I want you."

"And I was never one to disappoint a lady." His hard, perspiration-drenched body covered hers, found his mark and thrust forward.

So this is how it feels to fly, Maggie thought. Wrapping her legs around Jonah, she let him take her to the stars.

After this storm passed, she slept. Jonah lay by her side, studying her peaceful face. He had known it would be like this. From the minute he had kissed her, he had known her sweet facade hid a fire storm of passion. And he'd been right about once not being enough. Or even twice. Already he wanted her again.

"But it'll keep," he murmured, trailing a finger down Maggie's cheek. She stirred in her sleep, snuggling closer to him. He let his body relax against hers. "It'll keep. Because we'll both be here tomorrow."

Suddenly panic shook him fully awake. Maggie and tomorrow were two concepts he had been afraid to lump together. He resolved to make a fast getaway in the morning.

But when he awoke, Maggie's smile was the first thing he saw. Her touch, drifting low across his stomach, was the first thing he felt.

And leaving was the last thing on his mind.

Eight

Maggie's pancakes were thick and buttery-tasting. She served them with warmed honey. Jonah decided they should eat them in bed. So they spent their first full morning as lovers that way. With pancakes and honey in bed. The combination had possibilities she had only dreamed off. Maggie supposed her favorite eyelet-lace cotton sheets were ruined.

However, she also thought a couple of stains were a small sacrifice for so much pleasure.

It was the most decadent day of her life. She cancelled her weekly lunch with Liz and Cassandra, plus two other appointments, and turned on her answering machine.

Pretending to be hoarse from a terrible sore throat, Jonah reported in to the office. His mother must have given him a hassle, because he flashed Maggie a wicked smile and said, "It's okay, Mom. Maggie's taking care of me. Feeding me honey."

She waited until he was off the phone to throw a pillow at him, and they ended up on the floor rolling around like children on a playground. But their play was very adult. And extremely satisfying.

Eventually Jonah begged for some sleep. "To rest my poor bum leg," he said, grinning.

Slumbering away a Friday afternoon with him was just fine with Maggie. It was heaven having him in her bed, with his firm, male body wrapped tight around hers. Waking up late that afternoon was even better. She liked turning over and into his arms. She liked the scrape of his mustache against her cheek. The way he stretched like a lazy, satiated tomcat. The taste of his honey-flavored kiss.

She knew without a doubt that this was the way she always wanted to wake up. Morning. Noon. Or night. She wanted to be the first thing Jonah saw when he opened his eyes.

It was an impossible wish, however, and some of the sadness she was feeling must have shown in her eyes, because Jonah frowned.

"What's the matter?"

Maggie told him half the truth. "I was just wishing today could last a little longer."

"It isn't over."

"The sun's going down."

"But I feel like it's morning." He took her hand and placed it low on his stomach, against his erection. They smiled into each other's eyes. "Lady, you must have put some kind of miracle drug in those pancakes."

"I wish I had. We could market it and get very, very rich. Women all across America would be feeding their men pancakes for every meal."

Laughing, he pushed her onto her back and settled himself along her side. "I assure you the men wouldn't object. I haven't had a day quite like this in..." He paused. "Come to think of it, I've never had a day like this."

She kissed the corner of his mustache. "Neither have I."

Jonah put his face against Maggie's warm, fragrant neck. She smelled like flowers, as always. Flowers and pancakes and sex. It was a strangely erotic mixture. But then everything since the moment he had kissed her last night had been erotic. He could get used to nights and days like this. Moments like this.

The stirring of his body was more languid than insistent, and instead of acting on his arousal he turned his head to really look at the fast darkening room for the first time. The decor was so typically Maggie. Feminine, yes, but comfortable. Maybe a few too many ruffles, but the brass bed was nice. The oak dresser looked like an antique. So did the table beside the bed. And the picture frame on it.

Jonah's eyes narrowed as he stared at the photograph in that frame. He pushed himself up and reached across Maggie for it.

"Rachel?" he whispered.

Maggie nodded. "Barry took that the day we came home from the hospital."

Jonah sat up, leaning against the headboard as he looked down at the Maggie in this photograph. She didn't look so very different from now, really. Her hair had been long then. And she was perhaps a little heavier. But her face hadn't lost its look of innocence. Even if she had lost her child and her marriage since then.

The baby he couldn't tell much about. She looked small and red, the way most babies looked to Jonah. But there was no mistaking the love Maggie had for her. It poured out at him.

Very carefully he set the frame back on the bedside table. That picture told him everything Maggie wanted in life.

"Why haven't you married again?" he asked.

Maggie fluffed the pillows behind her back and settled beside Jonah, tucking the sheet modestly under her arms. She sighed. "You've asked me this before."

"I know you didn't want to repeat your first mistake, but . . ." He shrugged.

"You act as if marriage is something you just fall into."

"Isn't it?"

"Spoken like someone who has never been tempted."

"But you would like to be married."

She didn't try to deny that. "I want the right kind of marriage. I don't want to try it the other way again."

"Barry didn't do much to help you after Rachel died, did he?" Jonah asked with a sudden flash of insight.

"I can't really blame him. I closed in on myself for a while. When I came back to the real world, he had drifted away."

"For better for worse, in good times and bad," Jonah murmured. "Funny how people forget those vows, isn't it?"

Maggie smiled gently. "When you repeat those words, your head is full of dreams. Reality is a little harder to deal with."

"Very true. I've watched some marriages crumble in the face of reality."

She glanced at him sharply. "Really? Whose?"

"Guys like me," he said, with a careless sweep of his hands. "They're always on the move. They bring their wives with them when they can, at first. And then there are kids, and she stays behind and soon he's on his own. After a while there's no marriage left."

"Surely you've seen some relationships work under those same circumstances."

"Precious few."

The flat, dismissing tone of his voice told her everything he thought about marriage. He didn't believe it was the right choice for people like him. Of course that didn't surprise her but, still, the knowledge stung.

Jonah shook his head, started to ask Maggie another question and then realized what he was doing. He was lying in bed with a woman, discussing marriage. *Damnation*. From the minute he had met her he had been breaking all of his carefully set rules. This had to end. But how?

He considered getting up and finding an excuse to leave. One more look into Maggie's soft brown eyes told him that wouldn't do, however. What he did instead was kiss her. He kissed her and touched her and slid himself once again into her body. By keeping his mind and his body occupied with what he should be doing in bed, perhaps he could stay out of trouble.

Trouble, however, was what Jonah was in.

He knew it. He accepted that he had allowed himself to become hopelessly tangled up in Maggie. But he tried hard not to worry about where it all was leading as the days spun by. Perfect days. Full of crisp, autumn weather and the beginnings of a southern winter. Bright days. Cold nights. And Maggie.

For the first time in his life, Jonah saw the advantages to having someone to come home to. There were the back rubs, the good things she produced in her kitchen, the little things Maggie did that made him instantly comfortable. Most of all, there was the company. Being with her was never boring. She was happy with silences. She was just as pleased to launch into a full-fledged debate. Oh, there were times when she pushed a little too hard to make a point, especially about his brother, but largely she was easy to be with.

Easy to love.

Jonah first said those words to himself on Thanksgiving Day. They had been invited to Eugenia's for dinner, but Maggie had chosen instead to accompany him to his grandmother's. The clan had gathered for its usual feast and, if possible, Jonah thought they had grown in the month since his last visit. He counted two new babies among the cousins.

He wasn't surprised to see Maggie with one of those babies in her arms. She cooed and fussed and carried on like most women did about newborns. Even if he didn't know she had once had a child, he would have found her behavior very natural. What shocked him was how the sight of Maggie with a baby punched him in the gut. He had this moment, a blinding moment, of wanting to see her with his child, one they had made together. The entire room went dark as he admitted that urge. His legs weakened. His skin grew clammy.

He couldn't imagine what had brought on such a sudden, sharp yearning. Except perhaps that he loved Maggie.

Loved her.

The feeling took hold of him with all the ferociousness of a pit bull's locked jaw. He couldn't get rid of it. Not that day. Or all the next week.

He told himself it was merely sex. Maggie was an incredible lover. Willing, open, giving. She didn't share herself in half measures. And he wanted all she had to offer. Each time they made love it was a new experience. A different kind of high. Even when it was simple, hard and fast, he found a new sensation to savor. Experienced though Jonah was, he had never lost himself so completely in one woman.

The problem was that he couldn't separate the way he felt about Maggie in bed from the way he felt about her out of bed. That had been the trick until now. Before this, the women he had been involved with, even the two he had spent some serious time with, had been two-dimensional to Jonah. He dated them. He slept with them. There was no interweaving of lives. If he wanted to be friends with a woman, that was another matter. Jonah knew many women he regarded as pals. They were never those who aroused the least bit of sexual interest.

But Maggie was everything. His friend. His lover. She had thrown out her net, and he had jumped right in. Now how was he going to get out? Did he really want to get out?

He was ready to escape from Nashville, if not from Maggie. The restless part of him—the part of his make-up he had once been able to accept without a qualm—was stirring. His body had healed and he was ready to go back to work. As for the family business, well, Jonah was about to give up on that. He had taken Maggie's advice and managed to let go of some of his guilt about letting his father down. As she had said, he really couldn't change the past. And even though he and Michael had stopped shouting at each other, Jonah knew he couldn't do anything about the present, either. Michael was going to do what he wanted to do with the business, whether Jonah liked it or not. And that was really Michael's prerogative, anyway.

No, the only thing holding him here was Maggie. No one had ever held Jonah before, and he found it an unusual sensation, one he half loved, half hated.

His boss called the second week of December. They had a new project for him in Africa, a real challenge if it turned out as they described it. They would need him on the job sometime in February. Would he be free by then? Jonah could have said yes without giving his brother or the family firm a thought. But when he paused to consider Maggie, he asked for some time to make a decision. And he told no one about the call.

He toyed with the thought of asking her to go with him. That was another of his unbreakable rules. But he was giving it serious consideration on the night in mid-December when he and Maggie went to Liz and Nathan's new home for dinner.

Maggie had used jades and mauves as the key colors throughout the condominium. Pure white walls formed the background. For the furnishings, she had juxtaposed the antiques Liz favored with Nathan's sleek, modern pieces. The result was a somewhat disconcerting but altogether pleasing combination.

The spacious home perfectly reflected the personalities of its owners. Liz, as Jonah had discovered, was a selfless crusader. Her husband, who was president of his own public-relations firm, was unabashedly ambitious. Like their marriage, their new home was a balancing act.

A quite successful act, Jonah thought as he watched Nathan and Liz fix before-dinner drinks at the bar in their living room. He could feel the electricity when they so much as smiled at each other. Sometimes when he saw these two together, he felt as if he had mistakenly opened a door marked Do Not Disturb. They were that happy, that involved with each other.

Was the way he felt about Maggie as easy for others to see? Could she see it? Perhaps. He could see she was in love with him. It showed when she touched him. He had heard it in her sigh when they made love. It was as simple and as complex as the way she slipped her hand into his. He knew it could shatter like glass. Maggie's love was an awesome responsibility.

From his seat on Liz and Nathan's sofa, he watched her rearrange some pottery bowls on a low shelf near the wide front window. "Still decorating, I see."

"Liz keeps moving these," Maggie retorted.

"I do not," Liz replied. "It's the cat."

As if on cue, a gray tabby slunk out from under the Christmas tree and wound itself around Liz's legs.

Maggie laughed. "Liz, if you let the cat knock these bowls off this shelf, you will have lost a pretty hefty investment."

"Oh, she wouldn't knock them off." Liz stooped to croon to the cat, "You just don't like the way Auntie Maggie arranged those pretty bowls, do you, Kitty?"

"Sometimes I think we've arranged the entire house to suit the cat." Nathan laughed and settled into a wing chair.

Maggie sat down on the sofa next to Jonah. "I'm still amazed that you two have a cat."

"It's no more amazing than Cassandra having a baby." Liz perched on the arm of Nathan's chair.

"Cheaper, too," Nathan added.

Jonah was happy to see Maggie laughing about Cassandra. Her jealousy about the other woman's pregnancy had passed. In fact, just yesterday she had come home with a bag full of clothes and toys, Christmas gifts for a child who wouldn't be born for another six months.

The cat had transferred its attention to Maggie. She scratched it behind the ears and asked, "You two are going to make me an aunt to something other than this creature, aren't you?"

Liz sighed. "Someday. Soon, we hope. But right now there just isn't time for it. Between my caseload and Nathan's work, we have to schedule time with each other. I'm not sure where a baby would fit in."

"Well, at least now you have a place to live that you both like," Maggie said.

"And believe me, that can make all the difference in a marriage," Liz said. "Maggie, we will be eternally grateful for how you pulled this place together for us."

"It's my job."

"It's more than that." Liz turned to Jonah. "Maggie has this talent for making spaces—empty rooms—into a home. It's more than color or furniture. She creates places where people want to stay forever."

Jonah knew that about her, of course. He fit into Maggie's comfortable home all too well. He nodded and cast a glance around the room. "She certainly did well here."

Nathan nodded. "Yes, now I have a home and a mortgage. I feel really and truly married."

"But not as married as Daniel." Liz chuckled delightedly. "Cassandra told me he's looking at station wagons. Shaggy dogs are probably next on his list."

Nathan laughed heartily. "I'm afraid being an expectant father has given Daniel a case of Fred MacMurrayitis. But we shouldn't worry until he produces an uncle named Charlie who moves in to help raise the baby."

Everyone but Maggie laughed. "Now you guys just stop," she ordered. "If my brother wants to throw himself into the role of a family man, then I think it's grand. He's just living out the great American dream."

Her dream, Jonah thought, listening with only half a mind to the continuing laughter and talk. It was easy to see Maggie with a carload of kids on their way to baseball practice and dance lessons. She would bring them home to a big, old house. The curtains would be ruffled, tied back from the open windows. She would have a dog and a cat and a couple of goldfish, too. It would be so ordinary and so right. It was what she deserved. What she needed. She would miss part of that if she went with him.

No matter how much he loved her, he couldn't ask her to give up another dream. She had lost too many already.

Sipping his drink, Jonah eased back on the sofa and stared at the multicolored lights on Liz and Nathan's Christmas tree. Tonight, instead of asking Maggie to go with him to Africa, he would tell her he was leaving.

Just as he had made up his mind, Cassandra and Daniel arrived. Daniel was swinging a set of car keys and grinning. "Guess what, guys?"

"You bought a station wagon," Liz and Nathan and Maggie said in unison.

Jonah joined in the laughter at Daniel's discomfitted expression, but the evening had lost its charm for him.

Maggie knew something was bothering Jonah. He was quiet during dinner, and he wanted to leave soon after.

They didn't talk on the way home. Back at her apartment she gave him space. He would tell her what the problem was in his own time. While he stoked the fire, she changed into a gown and robe and settled into her chair to read.

She had grown used to having Jonah here all the time. A tiny voice in her heart kept whispering that maybe he would stay, that maybe he loved her just a little. She could ignore that voice most of the time. Not tonight, though. Tonight she pretended to read but watched Jonah instead.

He knelt in front of the fire, poking at logs that didn't need any stirring. Beneath his shirt, the muscles of his back moved with fluid beauty. He pushed easily to his feet, went to the kitchen and poured himself his habitual shot of tequila.

"You're barely limping at all," Maggie said, finally giving up the pretense and shutting her book. "How's your leg feeling?"

"Almost good as new."

"I guess you're glad."

He took a seat in the chair beside hers and rested both legs on the ottoman. She couldn't help but remember the first time he had sat there. Now she simply thought of the chair as his. It would always be his. Even after he left.

"You know, Maggie," he said slowly. "I came back to Nashville for two reasons. To get well and to help Michael."

A dizzying swirl of panic cut through her chest. "Yes. And now you're well, but the business—"

"Isn't going to change whether I stay or not."

She swallowed and looked down. She opened and closed her book once or twice and jumped when a spark from the fire flew against the fire screen. The silence dragged on for minutes. *Say it,* she wanted to scream at him. *Go ahead and say you're leaving.*

Jonah couldn't do it. Just looking at the tight set of Maggie's jaw made him feel guilty. He couldn't say he was leaving. Not now. Not yet. But he had to prepare her for when he would.

"Come here," he whispered, holding out his hand.

She slipped onto his lap, curling against his chest. He brushed his chin across her soft hair and took a deep breath of Maggie. Her scent had no name but that for him. It was simply her.

At last he found a place in which to start. "The last month has been really special, Maggie." She went stiff in his arms. *God, but this was so hard.* He wanted to stop but forged ahead. "I want you to know how important you will always be to me."

"Important?"

"You are the most giving, the sexiest woman I've ever known. I just..." He paused, not sure of what to say. "You should know...I mean I don't want to hurt you, Maggie. I'm afraid maybe I already have."

She twisted round to face him. "What do you mean, Jonah? What are you trying to say?"

He took her hand and turned it palm up and brought it to his lips. Eyes closed, he held it there for a moment, then looked at her again. He had to say something. "We did what I said we shouldn't do. We got involved. And it's been—" he drew a breath, wondering how to describe heaven "—it's been fabulous. But I don't want you to...to think—"

"You don't want me to think it's anything more than sex, right?" Maggie suggested in a small, strained voice.

"Of course it's more than that," he protested. "But it's not anything...it's not what you want, Maggie. It could never be what you want."

She wondered how he was so sure of what she wanted. Would he be surprised if she said all she required for happiness was him? Probably not surprised. But dismayed, surely. Men who came and went the way Jonah liked to do didn't care for complications such as love.

Maggie wanted to be a complication. She wanted...oh, sweet heaven, she wanted everything with this man. But it wasn't going to happen. And she had known that from the start.

If she had entertained any notions about changing him, well, notions were all they had been. At heart she was a practical woman. People don't change. Once, long ago, when she was a young, heartbroken mother, she had tried to change her husband, to make him into the sort of caring, sensitive person she needed. She had failed, and she had learned a lesson from that. She wouldn't try again.

Absently she fingered one of the buttons on Jonah's shirt. The threads were hanging loose. She could easily sew it on, but she chided herself for the thought. "Are you leaving?" she asked, as evenly as she could. Tears were filling her eyes.

Asking God to forgive him, Jonah lied to her. He shook his head and gathered her close. Without another word, they went to bed. He made love to her, as slowly, as sweetly as he could. He wanted his actions to say what he couldn't. That he loved her.

Maggie did her best to memorize each touch, each sigh. *This is all there is,* she told herself. *This is all there's ever going to be.*

Nine

He wanted to go. Yet he wanted to stay.

Jonah had never faced such a dichotomy of thinking. All of his life he had been sure—sure of where he wanted to be, of what he wanted to do. Now Maggie had changed all of those certainties to confusion.

Of course it wasn't really Maggie's fault. It was his. He had opened himself to her. He should have run away the first time he saw her.

Maggie, for her part, seemed unaware of the turmoil raging inside him. She never again asked him if or when he was leaving. She was so damn accepting that it almost made him angry. But just almost.

He told himself he should be withdrawing from her little by little, but he couldn't back away from her smile or her company or the passion they shared. They still managed to laugh together. They went to Christmas parties and had their own private celebrations. It was the silly, simple moments Jonah decided he liked best. The kissing under the mistletoe, hanging wreaths, hiding gifts from each other. Maggie made a special event out of a season he had grown used to ignoring.

During those special moments, he thought he might be content to settle down with her. It might be fine, at least for a while. But what about after the newness wore off? After the keenest edge of their passion for each other had dulled? He was certain his lifelong restlessness would rise in him and breed unhappiness. And what then? He couldn't see himself dragging Maggie away from her beloved hearth and home, from her friends and family. And he couldn't see himself staying, his discontent growing with every passing day. He wouldn't do that to Maggie or to himself.

A week before Christmas, before he could consider his decision any longer, he called his boss to talk again about the assignment in Africa. Jonah got excited just hearing about the project. He felt that familiar itch to be off to parts unknown, and he agreed to be there in February. About two months from now.

On the one hand, it seemed like an eternity to wait. Yet when he thought of Maggie, it didn't seem like enough time at all. It would pass so quickly. Too quickly.

After making the call, he stared at the telephone on his desk. He was trying to assimilate what he had just done when there was a knock on the frame of his open office door.

"Busy?" Michael said, coming inside.

Jonah shook his head. He should probably tell Michael now that he would be leaving, getting out of his hair. But no, maybe Maggie should be the first to know. With a frustrated sigh, Jonah sat back in his chair.

Michael paced around the office like a zoo animal stalking a cage. He pushed his hands in and out of his pockets. For the first time since Jonah had come home, Michael looked like the younger brother he had left here in Nashville over twelve years ago. His shirtsleeves were rolled up. And his blue eyes were clear of anger or resentment. He actually met Jonah's gaze, something he hadn't done in a long, long time, even though they had been getting along much better. However, he did look troubled.

"What's wrong?" Jonah asked him.

"Can you come in my office?"

"Sure." Almost afraid to know what was up, Jonah followed him down the hall.

Michael's office had once been their father's. It wasn't a particularly impressive room. The furniture was scarred from years of use. The off-white walls needed a coat of paint. The beige carpet could bear replacement. The room's greatest virtue was its size. It was big enough to hold a desk and files and the large rectangular table where their father had conducted meetings. This was where Jonah had decided to become an engineer. He could remember sitting with his father here, looking over charts and survey data, intrigued by the concept of turning an idea into a plan and the plan into reality. The room even smelled the same—like dust and cigar smoke.

On the table now there were several piles of paper— Jonah counted seven. They were neatly stacked, one right after the other down the table. Michael patted the first one. "It's all here," he told Jonah. "Each of these stacks represents one of our current projects."

Jonah just looked at him, frowning. What was Michael doing?

"I've included the original estimates, the plans, the current status—" he grinned wryly "—the problems and the list of subcontractors for each job, the estimate of how much money we're losing on each—"

"Wait a minute, Michael—"

"Let me finish, okay, Jonah?"

Jonah forced himself to be silent.

Michael sucked in his breath and ran a hand through his hair. The gestures were familiar to Jonah. Michael had always made a production out of any announcement, however major or minor. It was reassuring to see that hadn't really changed. Finally he released his long-held breath and said, "Jonah, I need your help."

Jonah stared at him in amazement. All these weeks, he had been trying to reach this moment. And now here it was, as simple as those five words. He was tempted for a moment to yell at Michael, to ask him why it had taken him so long to stop being a chump. But he knew that sort of attitude would prove nothing. So what he did was pull out a chair and reach for the first stack of papers.

"Well?" he asked and nodded at the chair beside him. "Aren't you going to sit down? Let's see if *we* can't figure a way out of this company's mess."

They worked until late that night. And the next, too. A haze of smoke settled over the table as they shifted schedules around. They factored costs. Figured and refigured the bottom line.

As they worked, they talked; and Jonah discovered the problems were what he had suspected all along. They had too many projects going for Michael to supervise them personally in the way their father had. The jobs were bigger and more complicated, for the most part. Michael hadn't trusted the subcontractors to do their jobs. He hadn't allowed anyone in his own operation to act autonomously. The end result was that Michael had fallen further and further behind. He had needed someone to share the big decisions with. Jonah should have been doing that instead of supervising mall parking lots and shuffling papers. Pride had kept Michael from asking for his help.

Michael's explanation was simple. "You came in here acting like a big shot," he told Jonah late on the second night of their work session. "I was losing my mind with worry. I was run ragged by details, but you acted as if you could run this little company with one hand tied behind your back. It made me angry."

Just as Maggie had said, Jonah thought. He ground out his cigar in an ashtray and paused to drain a paper cup of bitter, lukewarm coffee. "I guess I was trying to play big brother."

"The same role you've always played."

"I'm sorry," Jonah said simply. "I wish you had told me how you felt."

Michael's laugh was short. "I didn't think you would listen. You kept telling me what I should do. You kept insisting that you knew what Dad would have done." He leaned his elbows on the table and rubbed bloodshot eyes. "I've only been trying to do what Dad said he wanted."

That made Jonah pause. "You have?"

"We had started this expansion when he died. Surely you can see that." Michael tapped a column of figures on the yellow legal pad in front of him. "Dad wanted to go big-time. He said it was time he made his move or quit."

"Did Mom know about his plans?"

Michael shrugged. "I guess so. But you know she left the big decisions up to him, Jonah. She was here. She had responsibilities. But when it came right down to it, Dad was boss. After he died, she turned to me." His broad shoulders slumped, as if they had too many burdens to carry.

Jonah felt ashamed of himself. In the past few months he had only been concerned about his own reaction to their father's death. It had never occurred to him to think of how Michael had felt. He had lost his father and his senior business partner. Trying to pick up the slack must have been an incredible strain.

"I went full speed ahead with the plans Dad and I had made," Michael continued. "I went too far, too fast. I guess I wanted the big time, too. For Dad." His gaze shifted away from Jonah's. "And for reasons of my own."

"What was wrong?" Jonah cuffed Michael on the shoulder, turning what could have been a heavy moment into something less intense. "Were you tired of being Roger Pendleton's son, Jonah Pendleton's brother?"

"You're damn right I was." A slight smile twisted Michael's mouth. "But I'm surprised you figured that out."

Maggie had been the one to figure it out, but Jonah didn't want to go into that with Michael. They had to start formulating a plan to get things on track with the company.

"With two of us working together, maybe we can salvage something," Michael said.

Jonah realized that now was the time to tell Michael he would be leaving soon. But there was something of the boy Michael had been in the man's face. An expectant look, the same one he had worn on those Sundays when they had played at Grandmother P's. Jonah had been the one who had led expeditions into the woods. He had planned tree houses and designed bridges. Michael had followed at his heels. That wasn't the way it would be now. Michael was his own man. If he would think clearly, logically and worry less about expansion and more about maintaining what was already in progress, he could get through this crisis. But he needed, *he had asked for* Jonah's help. Jonah was afraid that if he said he was leaving, Michael would close him out again. He couldn't let that happen.

He could cancel out on the African project, of course, and stay even longer. But even as Jonah considered that possibility, the itch to move on settled in his gut again. He looked around the familiar, cluttered office. He loved this place. But he had never planned on getting stuck here. He would help Michael only as long as he could.

So he told his brother nothing. Together they worked out an ambitious plan to get Pendleton Construction out of trouble. Jonah thought if he worked very hard and everything went their way, Michael would be able to handle things on his own by February.

Christmas and New Year's came and went, and despite the sadness in Maggie's heart they were special times because Jonah was still by her side. He didn't talk about leaving. She didn't ask questions. She had accepted that all he could give her was the warmth of his body and this little piece of his life. She tried to be content with that.

Her only problem was the occasional flash of hope he gave her. He and Michael were working together, at last, and there was an interaction between the men she hadn't seen before. A camaraderie. Carrie seemed relieved. They even had a few family dinners, with Jonah and Maggie, Michael and his wife and daughters. Maggie felt like such a part of the group, like Jonah's partner. She fought the feeling and told herself not to grow too comfortable. He was making no promises. Unfortunately that didn't keep her from praying that he would.

January's weather was mild for the most part, but an Arctic cold front moved through Nashville during the last week. They had a trace of snow, and Maggie had to skirt ice patches in the parking lot of the restaurant where she always met Liz and Cassandra for their weekly lunches.

She was surprised to find both of them waiting for her. She was usually the first to arrive, and Cassandra was habitually late.

"Pregnancy must be having a settling effect on you." Maggie draped her coat around the back of her chair and then patted Cassandra's arm. "You're on time."

"The only thing that's settling is my tummy," Cassandra replied. "And it's becoming a big, round ball."

With a shake of her head, Liz set down her coffee cup. "No one can even tell you're pregnant. You don't need those maternity clothes you're wearing."

"But I can't wear my regular clothes. My shape has changed completely." Cassandra turned to Maggie.

"Did you feel this way with Rachel—like a giant balloon?"

Laughing, Maggie nodded and drew off her soft black leather gloves. She and Cassandra had talked a great deal about the baby in recent months. It didn't hurt to discuss Rachel. Not the way it once had, anyway. Beside the way it had propelled her into Jonah's arms, Maggie thought her newfound peace about Rachel was the good thing that had come of her crisis on that night in mid-November. She had examined all of her feelings about Rachel's death, and she had cried her last tears over her loss.

After they had given their orders to the waitress, Liz sat forward, her expression conspiratorial. "I think Eugenia's going to marry Herbert."

Cassandra disagreed. "It'll never happen. Why should Eugenia marry anyone at this time in her life?"

"He's by her side all the time," Maggie pointed out.

"Jonah's by your side all the time, too," Cassandra said, her dark eyes dancing with mischief. "Does that mean you're getting married?"

Maggie concentrated on unwrapping her silverware and smoothing a pale pink napkin across her lap.

"Well?" Liz pressed.

"Jonah and I are not Eugenia and Herbert."

Cassandra chuckled. "Of course not. You're a whole lot likelier to end up tying the knot."

Maggie kept her voice even. "I wouldn't bet on it."

"But why?" Liz asked.

A giant lump appeared in Maggie's throat as she considered the question. *Why indeed?* She didn't know if she could explain it to her friends. They were sophisticated people, but she wasn't sure how they would react to the knowledge that Maggie, *dull, prudish Maggie*, was sleeping with a man whose intentions toward her were of the most temporary and superficial kind. If she told them she was in love with him, they would feel all the more sorry for her when he left. They knew so much about her life already. Sometimes she thought they knew too much. They certainly meddled enough, and she had been tired of that for a long time.

"Can we drop it?" she asked.

"Oh, come on," Cassandra wheedled. "We want to know, Maggie. Has it gotten serious? Are you sleeping with him?"

"Cassandra!" Liz protested, but there was lively interest in her eyes.

Though sex wasn't an unlikely subject for three people who had shared confidences for their entire lives, Maggie felt her cheeks grow warm. "I said I didn't want to talk about it, guys. Okay?"

Cassandra was not to be deterred. "But—"

"Would you please shut up?" The harshness of those words surprised even Maggie.

Cassandra sat back as if she had been slapped.

Concern had drawn Liz's delicate features into a frown. "Maggie? Is something wrong?"

Shaking her head, Maggie gathered up her gloves and purse. "I'm sorry," she told Cassandra. "I didn't mean to snap at you. I just need..." She drew a deep breath. "I need to leave." Without a backward glance, she got up, grabbed her coat and hurried through the crowded restaurant.

Outside she paused to pull the cold winter air into her lungs. It cleared her head, but it did nothing for the pain she had in the region of her heart. God, why couldn't they have left the subject of Jonah alone? They had only reminded her of how fragile her relationship with him was.

The need to see him was unbearable. He had told her that tonight he wanted to take her out to dinner. They were going to dress up, go dancing, paint the town, as he had put it. But Maggie didn't think she could wait until tonight to feel his arms around her. When he was touching her was the only time she felt whole.

She headed for his office, expecting to find him inside on a cold day such as this. What she didn't expect was the turmoil that greeted her when she reached the glassed front door.

It was almost like déjà vu, the way Michael and Jonah and Carrie stood in the reception area. Even the receptionist's avid expression was familiar. Things had looked just like this before, on another afternoon. Only that time, Jonah had argued with Michael. Now he stood rock-solid still, his back to the door.

"I should have known," Michael hurled at Jonah just as Maggie slipped inside. "I should never have trusted you. We made all these plans. You said you would help. And now you're leaving. You selfish bastard. You're leaving!"

Carrie said something then, but it was Michael's words that echoed through Maggie like gunshots, finding her heart. It felt as if it shattered in her chest. *Jonah was leaving.*

Dimly she heard him say, "I'll be here for another week or so."

"No, you won't," Michael snapped. "Get out now. And don't ever think you can come back."

Jonah turned around then. Maggie hated that, because she knew he saw how destroyed she was. *Damn, why did he have to see that?* Before he could see her tears, however, she turned and fled.

Ten

She had control of herself by the time Jonah got home. She sat at her kitchen table, hands folded, waiting for him when he opened the back door.

"I'm sorry," she said softly. "I was just surprised."

Awkwardly he shifted from foot to foot. "Maggie, I'm the one who's sorry. I was going to tell you tonight."

"When we went out."

"Yes."

She stood, feeling as if she moved like a robot. She crossed to the sink and filled the teakettle with water.

Why doesn't she say something? Jonah waited expectantly near the door, knowing at any moment Maggie was going to turn on him. She was going to scream and yell, and that was going to make it easier for him to leave. He should have known that wasn't her style. He should have realized it would never be easy to leave her.

When he spoke her name, she simply turned to look at him. And he knew this picture of her was the one he would carry in his heart forever.

For always, no matter where he traveled or how many years separated them, he knew he would be able to see Maggie as she was now—in a pink sweater, with winter sunshine in her blond hair and heartbreak in her brown eyes.

"Maggie." Her name was no more than a sigh on his lips as he pulled her into his arms.

"When?" she whispered against his chest.

"I'm going tomorrow."

She pulled back and looked up at him. "But you told Michael—"

"He wants me gone. It's better for—" he paused to draw a hand down her cheek "—for everyone if I leave."

Maggie wanted to hit him. She had rarely known a violent urge in her life, but she wanted to slap Jonah for the assumptions he had made about what was best for her. But as she had for a lifetime, she tamped down the urge. Instead she put her arms around him, and she pressed her face against the cold leather of his jacket. She breathed in the now familiar scent of his tobacco, and she lifted her face for his kiss.

Later that afternoon they made love. She wanted to capture every elusive second. She didn't want to forget the silky-rough texture of Jonah's hair. The exact color of his eyes. The way they darkened when she cupped his fullness in her hand. She recorded the sound of his voice in her head, knowing she would replay his sighs again and again. She was certain she would never forget the way he gasped when their bodies joined. Till she died she would taste the bitterness that flooded her mouth when she faced the complete reality of his leaving.

She had thought she was prepared for this moment. She had been rehearsing it for weeks. But now...now that she faced it, she was bitter and frustrated and angry.

Jonah left her in bed while he showered the next morning. Maggie feigned sleep and let anger churn through her. When his towel-draped figure appeared in the doorway from the bathroom, she sat up.

"You could stay," she told him.

The room was silent as he ran a hand through his damp hair. He bit his lip, looking as if he might say something. Instead he merely shook his head.

"You *should* stay," she insisted, her voice rising. Her whirling, panicked thoughts latched onto a reason. "For Michael."

"Maggie—"

"He needs you."

Jonah's tone was very hushed, very final. "I can't stay."

Something seemed to explode in her head, and for a moment red swam in front of her eyes. When it cleared, Maggie tossed back the covers and got out of bed. She jerked on her robe. "It isn't that you can't stay, Jonah. It's that you *won't*."

"You know—"

She turned on him. "I know nothing except that you're letting everyone down. Can't you put someone else's need before your own? You came home, thinking you would make yourself feel a little better by helping your brother. And now you run away again."

He took a step forward. "I'm not running."

Tears of rage scalded her eyes. "Aren't you?"

"I never said I would stay."

"And that makes it all right, doesn't it?" she jeered. "You come here and you get into people's lives, but it doesn't matter how you affect them, because you never make any promises. Except to yourself."

"That isn't true."

"Would it hurt to give Michael six months of your life?" she demanded. "It was okay to come home and demand to be a part of his life, but now that he wants you to stay that's too normal, isn't it? You're too concerned about riding off into the sunset like some mysterious drifter. That pose of yours is more important than anything."

Jonah came toward her. "Maggie, this is just me. This is no pose—"

"Oh, yes it is." She headed for the door, then wheeled to face him, the tears streaming down her face. "You make me sick, Jonah. You've had everything so easy. You've spent your life in the kind of family I would have killed for. Your parents loved you, gave your your blessing to do anything your heart desired. The only thing they forgot to teach you was the part about commitment, about responsibility. Michael was right yesterday. You really are just a selfish bastard."

"Maggie—"

"Someday you're going to hate yourself for what you're doing. But then it'll be too late."

She left him then, and Jonah stood in the middle of her room, water from his towel dripping onto her rug. He wasn't sure how long he remained motionless. Maggie's words echoed in his head. He tried to deny their truth, but he couldn't. And he decided it really was for the best that he was leaving. Because a selfish bastard was the last thing Maggie needed in her life.

Maggie huddled in a corner of her living-room sofa for at least an hour, not moving except to jump when Jonah slammed her back door on his way out. She went to her bedroom and stood in the doorway, staring at the empty hangers that swayed in the closet.

So he was gone.

Surprisingly all she could feel was anger. The hurt set in later that day. It intensified as the days passed.

She could only compare the pain to what she knew after Rachel's death. It was like a dense, dense fog. No one could reach her. Not Liz or Cassandra or her brother. She shut them out when they tried.

When she could no longer bear it, she ran to Eugenia. As she had done when she was a child, she put her head on the woman's shoulder and cried, begging her to say it was going to be all right.

Eugenia, who would have done anything to spare Maggie heartbreak, didn't give her any false hopes, either. All she could do was tell Maggie a story about a man and a woman, crazy in love with each other, planning to be married. Until the woman got cold feet and ran away. Maggie knew Eugenia was talking about herself.

"You see, I thought I had to be free," Eugenia explained. "I threw away Mark's love as casually as Jonah is throwing away yours. I traded it in on a chance at adventure, on a train ticket. And when I changed my mind, of course, it was too late. Mark was dead, and all I had were memories and regrets."

"I didn't think you regretted anything," Maggie whispered, surprised by the unshed tears in Eugenia's bright, blue eyes.

"Everyone has something he would change. The trick is to not grow bitter over it, to get on with your life."

"You're saying I should get on with mine, right? That I shouldn't dream about Jonah coming back?"

Tenderly Eugenia brushed a lock of hair from Maggie's forehead. "I couldn't tell you to stop dreaming, Maggie dear. You wouldn't, even if I did."

Eugenia's words were wise, though they brought Maggie little comfort. She went home, curled up in Jonah's chair and stared at the fire. Eventually she cried, hating herself for the weakness of tears. If only she could go back and do things differently. Especially their last, angry scene. In her mind she replayed every bitter word she had hurled at him. Some of it was true. But she shouldn't have gotten so angry. Their last minutes together should have been something to cherish.

Hugging her arms to her chest, she rocked back and forth, trying to stem the flood of tears and regrets.

The thump of something hitting the floor caught her attention. Then her name. She turned to find Jonah standing in the doorway. Not a dream. Jonah. A battered brown suitcase sat at his feet. His too long hair was windblown. His face was drawn and pale. His eyes full of trepidation.

Somewhat stunned, Maggie got to her feet. She started toward him, but was no further than the kitchen table when she caught herself. *No, she wouldn't run to him. Even though her heart was doing cartwheels, she would stop right here.* She clasped her hands together and waited.

"I *had* to come back," Jonah whispered hoarsely.

Just looking at him was too painful to bear, so Maggie shifted her gaze to his dusty brown boots. Words forced their way past the lump in her throat. "*Had* to?"

"Because I love you."

Those words were raw. They seemed to rip from deep inside Jonah. They brought Maggie's gaze spinning back to meet his, but still she couldn't move.

Feeling like a gambler who had played his last card, Jonah let his shoulders slump. "After the way I walked out of here, I guess admitting that I love you isn't enough."

Eyes wide and glimmering with tears, Maggie continued to stare at him. *What was she thinking? Didn't she believe what he was saying?*

Jonah brought his chin up, took a step forward and held out his hand. "Love has to be enough, Maggie. Because nothing in my life is right without you. Nothing. I love you too much to try living without you. I'll stay here until you believe that."

He didn't wait for her to move. Instead he caught her in his arms. "Tell me I can stay, Maggie. Please."

With a soft cry of thanksgiving she gathered him close. "Stay or go," she whispered. "I don't care where we are. Just make sure I'm with you, Jonah. Don't ever leave me again."

In his kiss she found all the reassurance she needed.

Much later they sat in front of the fire, and Jonah told Maggie about the last few days.

"I kept hearing what you said," he murmured. "I got on the plane, and your voice was roaring in my ear. I couldn't escape from the truth. I got off the plane in

Africa and realized I had to come right back home. To set things right."

"I'm sorry about some of what I said. I shouldn't—"

"No," he interrupted. "You were so right. My life has been easy. I have been selfish. Especially these past few months. I kept pretending I was making a big sacrifice in trying to win Michael's cooperation, in trying to help him. But I wasn't. I was doing it all for myself."

"To keep from feeling guilty about not being here for your father."

"And that was so dumb. Because my father didn't need me here."

Maggie smiled. "Oh, I'm sure he would have been pleased if you had decided to stay."

"I know he missed me. But I doubt he wasted much energy in wishing I was here. He was too busy pursuing his own dreams, the same as I was pursuing mine. He never would have wanted me to feel guilty." Jonah paused. "There is something I'm going to do for Dad, though."

"What?"

"I'm going to stay here and help Michael. He needs me."

Maggie frowned. "I'm sure he does need you, Jonah, but you can't stay if it's not really what you want to do, above and beyond what you feel you owe to Michael or to your father's memory. It's okay to be unselfish, but if you're going to resent the decision somewhere down the road, you won't be doing Michael any favors. You can't—"

"I know, I know," Jonah interrupted. "I've already been through that with Michael."

"You've seen Michael?"

"I went to him first. If he rejected me, I could deal with it. I was more afraid of your reaction."

Tenderly, Maggie touched his cheek. There was nothing for him to be afraid of now. He was home with her, where he belonged. "What did Michael say?" she prompted.

"We had a long talk. I'm staying because I want to stay. I want to see if I can put down some roots. I want to work on making a commitment. To you. You are going to marry me, aren't you?"

Her heart felt full enough to burst, but there was one thing she wanted to make very clear. "You don't have to stay here to make a commitment, Jonah. I meant it when I said you could stay or go. You and I can make a home anywhere—"

"That was the other thing that hit me when I got on the plane to come home. I realized that if you were by my side, I might not be feeling so lost. I just need to be with you. Anywhere on earth will be home if you're there with me."

"If you want to get back on that plane, I'll go with you," she insisted. "And we'll make it work. I can promise you that."

He nodded. "I'm sure of that. But let's stay here for a while. Let's have a wedding." His lips caught hers again. "Let's start working on a family. We're not gettin' any younger, you know."

Laughing, she laid her head against his chest. His heart beat close to her ear, reassuringly near. "I love you, Jonah."

"Do you realize that's the first time you've told me that?"

She looked up in surprise. "I guess I've been saying it in my heart for so long that I figured I must have told you."

"That's okay." He drew her lips back to his. "I'm going to be hearing it for a long time to come."

"For the rest of your life."

Jonah pulled away from the kiss before it could deepen. The love he felt for Maggie soared through him, but there was something he had to do before another moment passed. He got to his feet.

"Where are you going?"

"To call Eugenia." He grinned down at Maggie's amazed look. "I have to tell her I found it."

She still looked puzzled. "Found what?"

"The hidden prize." Tenderly he touched her cheek. "Your heart."

Epilogue

On Eugenia's shoulders, the sun was warm. The air was fresh, redolent with the scents of newly mown grass and flowers. The day was perfect, as only an April day in Nashville can be. What a wonderful day for a birthday party.

She tightened her grip on Herbert's arm as they walked across the lawn to the garden gazebo where the children were waiting to have tea with her.

"Now watch your step," he cautioned her.

She resisted the urge to tell him to watch his own step and smiled up at him sweetly. He was such a silly, dear old thing. She was eighty-seven today, and he was seventy-five, and he had proposed for what must have been the thousandth time this morning. As if they needed marriage at their age. Pooh! What a crazy idea. She loved him, yes, but she preferred things as they were.

The children came running out as they neared the gazebo. They clustered around her, laughing, jabbering about cake and ice cream and presents until their mothers came to shoo them inside.

"Oh, let them alone," Eugenia said.

Liz sighed. "If it were up to you, these children would run wild as young savages."

"And what harm could that do? They'll have to become civilized soon enough." Sniffing, Eugenia took her seat at the head of the table. Her bones ached a little, but otherwise she felt fine. Extremely well, considering.

She sat back and surveyed the scene in front of her. Three little ones were gathered at her table, wiggling and squirming and impatient for their cake. Two others were in high chairs. Five in all. Cassandra's son and daughter. Liz's little girl. Maggie's two boys. What fine, handsome children they were. As dear to her heart as their mothers were.

And their fathers, too. Looking up, Eugenia surveyed the men who had claimed the hearts of her treasures. Nathan, Daniel and Jonah. Each so different, so right for the women in their lives.

Those women...oh, but Eugenia loved them so. Filled with pride, she looked from one face to the other.

Here was Liz, still crusading for those less fortunate, and so happy with Nathan and their child. Eugenia hoped she was planning another child or two. If so, it was time she got busy. She would have to speak to her about that.

Cassandra, of course, didn't need any more children. Eugenia had told her so just the other day. She had enough on her hands with Daniel and her school and her two raven-haired scamps.

On the other hand, Maggie could most likely handle a half dozen young Pendletons. She was pregnant with her third now. About to have it, too, Eugenia thought, eyeing Maggie's rounded stomach. Jonah was going to bundle the whole family off to Australia after the baby was born. Eugenia thought she might just go with them. That was one continent she had never got around to visiting.

"*Madame*, the candles."

Realizing her mind had wandered, as it did sometimes these days, Eugenia glanced up at Jeannette. Dear, loyal Jeannette. Just where would she be without her old friend?

"Blow out the candles, 'Genia," Eric Pendleton said impatiently.

"Help me," Eugenia invited, and the children and adults gathered around. It would take everyone's breath to douse the blaze on this cake.

"Don't forget your wish," young Patrick O'Grady ordered.

Eugenia complied, shutting her eyes and wishing for eighty-seven more years. If not that, then at least enough time to make sure these children got everything they wanted from life.

While her eyes were still closed, someone edged onto her lap.

"Genie," Liz admonished her daughter as she came forward. "Now don't crawl all over your Aunt Eugenia."

"It's my birthday," Eugenia said. "And my namesake can do anything she wants."

Genie Hollister blinked her big, blue eyes and promptly poked at the diamond-and-sapphire brooch pinned to Eugenia's dress. "I want it," she demanded.

"And someday you shall have it, my darling," Eugenia promised her. "I'm going to give some of my treasures to all of you. Patrick will get my onyx ring. And Eric my favorite jade pin, and..."

Listening to her, the children's mothers looked at each other and smiled. Eugenia's jewelry would be a precious bequest, but her real gift to these children couldn't be measured. If they listened well to her, she would give them magic. And dreams. And faith in the strength of love.

And those were qualities to treasure.

*   *   *   *   *

SILHOUETTE *Desire*™

COMING NEXT MONTH

#565 TIME ENOUGH FOR LOVE—Carole Buck
Career blazers Doug and Amy Hilliard were *just too busy*...until they traded the big city winds for the cool country breezes and discovered the heat of their rekindled passion.

#566 BABE IN THE WOODS—Jackie Merritt
When city-woman Eden Harcourt got stranded in a mountain cabin with Devlin Stryker, she found him infuriating—infuriatingly *sexy*! This cowboy was trouble from the word go!

#567 TAKE THE RISK—Susan Meier
Traditional Caitlin Petrunak wasn't ready to take chances with a maverick like Michael Flannery. Could this handsome charmer convince Caitlin to break out of her shell and risk all for love?

#568 MIXED MESSAGES—Linda Lael Miller
Famous journalist Mark Holbrook thought love and marriage were yesterday's news. But newcomer Carly Barnett knew better—and together they made sizzling headlines of their own!

#569 WRONG ADDRESS, RIGHT PLACE—Lass Small
Linda Parsons hated lies, and Mitch Roads had told her a whopper. Could this rugged oilman argue his way out of the predicament...or should he let love do all the talking?

#570 KISS ME KATE—Helen Myers
May's *Man of the Month* Giles Channing thought Southern belle Kate Beaumont was just another spoiled brat. But beneath her unmanageable exterior was a loving woman waiting to be tamed.

AVAILABLE NOW:

Silhouette Romances™

DIAMOND JUBILEE CELEBRATION!

It's Silhouette Books' tenth anniversary, and what better way to celebrate than to toast _you_, our readers, for making it all possible. Each month in 1990, we'll present you with a DIAMOND JUBILEE Silhouette Romance written by an all-time favorite author!

Welcome the new year with _Ethan_—a LONG, TALL TEXANS book by Diana Palmer. February brings Brittany Young's _The Ambassador's Daughter_. Look for _Never on Sundae_ by Rita Rainville in March, and in April you'll find _Harvey's Missing_ by Peggy Webb. Victoria Glenn, Lucy Gordon, Annette Broadrick, Dixie Browning and many more have special gifts of love waiting for you with their DIAMOND JUBILEE Romances.

Be sure to look for the distinctive DIAMOND JUBILEE emblem, and share in Silhouette's celebration. Saying thanks has never been so romantic....

SRJUB-1